A Thirst in Babylon

William Neil Martin

BookLocker
Trenton, Georgia

Print ISBN: 978-1-958892-79-4
Ebook ISBN: 979-8-88531-739-9

Published by BookLocker.com, Inc., Trenton, Georgia.

BookLocker.com, Inc.
2024

First Edition

Library of Congress Cataloguing in Publication Data
Martin, William Neil
A Thirst in Babylon by William Neil Martin
Library of Congress Control Number: 2024908721

Books by
WILLIAM NEIL MARTIN

Fiction
CITIZENS OF EDEN
(No longer in print)

STORM SURGE

THE McALLISTER BRAND

A THIRST IN BABYLON

Non-fiction
NORTH OF RED ROCK CANYON
(No longer in print)

THROUGH THICK AND THIN
The Coming of Age of
Floyd and Christine Martin in
Southern Mississippi
1922 - 1952

Dedication

To my devoted wife, Marie
Thank you for your love and support.

MONDAY
March 12, 1928

10:00 A.M.

JEFF KIENAST CONTROLLED the Curtiss Jenny from the rear seat of the biplane as the aircraft flew a westerly course no more than three hundred feet above a terrain of scrub brush and occasional stands of stunted oak. The southern California sky was gray and sullen, which intensified the sense of gloom that was swelling within the young pilot. Though this was merely a sightseeing flight, his suspicions were growing that his passenger had a more sinister motive. He wished by all that was good and decent that he had never consented to having any involvement in what he was beginning to suspect was a villainous act.

The pilot frowned as he glimpsed at the gray-haired passenger who sat in the front seat of the plane. A growing disappointment in the man saddened the pilot – all the more so because the passenger was his uncle.

A series of ridges drifted downward from a distant rise several miles to the west by southwest, like huge fingers splayed out from an arthritic hand, forming canyons of various widths and depths. It was over one of these ridges that the plane flew, as Jeff banked the ten-year-old relic of the Great War to the left and followed a generally south by southwest course along the contours of San Francisquito Canyon. The canyon was narrow, and its walls rose steadily upward. In order to remain above the canyon, the pilot moved the yoke back slightly. The Jenny's 90-horsepower engine struggled to attain the higher altitude. The air speed dropped to 50 miles per hour and the pilot had to dip the nose slightly to regain speed. Even in straight and level flight a Curtiss Jenny JN-3 had a top speed of only 75 miles per hour. But Jeff could not take a chance on slowing the plane to a speed less than 50 for fear that it would stall, and, at that low altitude, the aircraft would crash into the canyon like a falling rock. After regaining a safe cruising speed, he nursed the stick back ever so gently until the plane gradually increased its altitude to approximately three hundred feet above the canyon's rim.

Fewer than ten minutes had passed when the plane flew over a perpendicular ridge that boxed the canyon, and beyond the ridge a narrow body of water, four miles in length, formed a lake inside the canyon. Regret ate away at Jeff as he realized the purpose of his mission that morning. His uncle had been a resident of the Owens Valley, located two hundred miles north of Los Angeles, and he was one of many from that region who contended that the water below had been stolen from Owens River and piped to this site by William Mulholland, Chief Engineer of the Los Angeles Water Company. And it was his desire to put an end to this theft – by whatever means. Belatedly, it then dawned on the young pilot – this was not a sightseeing aerial tour of the new dam. It was a reconnaissance mission!

Something had been gnawing at him throughout the flight. His uncle was not given to sightseeing tours. There was a sinister nature about him, but over the years the pilot had tried to ignore that fact. Aside from Jeff's father, this man was the only relative he had.

Shortly after the plane was directly over the lake Jeff noticed a stone structure on the rim of the canyon, off to his left. According to the map that had been provided prior to his departure, the structure was the water company's Power

Station Number One. Two large pipes, several feet in diameter, descended from the side of the power plant down the bank of the canyon and into the water.

A short time later, as Jeff flew the plane on its course, the top of the dam came into view directly in front of him. It was the dam that his passenger wanted to get a good look at, so he slowed his speed as much as he dared. Rather than decreasing the power on the throttle, he simply raised the nose of the plane slightly and there was an immediate slowing of the aircraft.

As the plane neared the dam it became quite clear that the lake was full, for the water level was up to the top of the massive structure. The water was rough that morning, for Jeff could see whitecaps even from his altitude. It appeared that some were even sloshing over the top of the dam. Of course, that might have been his imagination, because his focus was not on whitecaps, but on the man who was standing atop the rampart in the center of the span that crossed the canyon. Jeff extended an arm and waved to the man, but the wave was not returned. The man on the rampart merely stared upward, his gaze following the plane as it flew over the dam and over the canyon beyond the lake. The passenger showed no reaction to the man atop the dam.

With the dam behind him, Jeff dipped the nose of the aircraft, and the Jenny regained its cruising speed. Less than a mile south of the dam the plane flew over a narrow outgrowth of rock that jutted out from the east wall like a small promontory, causing the canyon to veer sharply to the right. On the other side of the outcropping, which was no more than fifty yards wide at its base, the floor of the canyon proceeded east for a short distance then returned to its generally southern course. At the apex of the curve, resting at the base of the canyon's eastern bank, was Power Station Number Two. It appeared to be a twin of Station Number One.

It was somewhere in this area, he had been told, off to the west of the canyon, that the popular western screen star Harry Carey had a three-thousand-acre working ranch. The thought crossed his mind that, if, by any chance the dam should break, would the Carey ranch be protected from any flood damage?

Beyond the power station the canyon widened in places, and the sight below brought a sudden shock that sent a wave of nausea from the pit of Jeff's stomach. On the ground beneath were several modest residences! There was even what appeared to be a schoolhouse atop the earthen floor that separated the walls of the canyon. This was something he had not anticipated. There was an actual community directly beneath him – with families – a schoolhouse – *children*! He had not expected to find people living within these canyon walls! If the dam broke, a hundred-foot wall of water would be on this little community in a fraction of a minute!

Jeff leaned forward and tapped his passenger on the shoulder. When the uncle turned his head toward him, the pilot pumped his hand downward several times, his index finger extended, to emphasize what was below them. The passenger briefly glanced down at the community and shrugged. This angered Jeff, but there was nothing he could do at the moment.

Two more minutes of flight and the biplane reached the mouth of the canyon, which formed a rather rugged T-intersection with the gentle flow of the Santa Clara River. The pilot banked the plane to the right and headed west, following the riverbed a few more miles until coming upon the north/south highway commonly known as the Ridge Route. At the highway Jeff banked again to the right and followed a northerly course above the highway, slowly increasing the plane's altitude.

The Santa Clara River continued under the highway bridge in a westerly course, its banks cutting through the countryside, entering Ventura County, and passing through such towns as Camulos, Piru, Fillmore, Santa Paula and Saticoy, eventually emptying into the Pacific Ocean between Oxnard and Ventura, fifty miles west of San Francisquito Canyon.

After completing his bank to the right, Jeff looked down over Castaic Junction, where he saw two people, a boy in his late teens and a grown man, below and slightly to his left. The man was working on a Model T touring car behind a motor court, and the boy appeared to be helping him. The man was preoccupied with the car's engine, but the boy looked up and waved enthusiastically as the low-flying biplane flew over. Jeff managed a half-smile and returned the wave, but his mind was elsewhere – back in the canyon – focused on the numerous residences and the school in San Francisquito Canyon, clearly within the flood path of the dam. He could not get the thought of all those innocent people out of his mind, nor could he understand the obvious indifference exhibited by his passenger. The growing knot persisted in the pit of his stomach, and he fought back the bile that rose in his throat, trying desperately not to vomit.

On the ground the boy followed the flight path of the aircraft, which continued to climb to a higher altitude as it proceeded north, parallel with the highway, for another minute. It then banked to the right and flew a somewhat north by northeast course. The teenager continued to watch the plane until it disappeared into the gloomy skies. More than an hour would pass before the Curtiss Jenny touched down at its point of origin, a runway of hard-packed sand on the northern edge of Mojave.

HALF AN HOUR after the plane flew over him at such a frighteningly low altitude, Tony Harnischfeger was still standing atop the rampart of the St. Francis Dam. This was not a good day for him, and that blasted plane just added to the drama. He would not be surprised, he thought, if the Old Man had hired that pilot to fly over just to check up on him. Then again, that wouldn't make much sense, seeing as the Old Man was on his way right this minute to see him about the condition of the dam.

Harnischfeger had been hired as the damkeeper when the dam first opened almost two years earlier. He lived with his common-law wife and small son in a cottage provided for them a quarter of a mile downstream from the structure. Prior to his employment as keeper of the dam, Harnischfeger worked as a security guard patrolling the Los Angeles Water Company's aqueduct that ran from Owens Valley to Los Angeles. His patrolling area was in Jawbone Canyon, an isolated piece of high desert country north of the town of Mojave. He and his small family had resided in the nearby community of Cantil.

The security measures taken by the water company were certainly justified, because there had been attempts to sabotage the aqueduct. On more than one occasion a group of raiders, purportedly from the Owens valley, dynamited sections of the aqueduct, causing significant damage. It was for this reason that armed patrols were employed.

Just before the St. Francis Dam opened in 1926, Tony Harnischfeger was offered the job of damkeeper, and he jumped at the chance. For him it was quite a promotion. In addition to the pay increase, the water company provided living quarters for him and his family.

After two years, however, the novelty of the new job had worn off, and he had developed a strong sense of apprehension about this concrete behemoth that had become his charge. The truth be known, it was more than apprehension. Harnischfeger had a genuine fear of the dam. He frequently had nightmares of him and his family sleeping in the small cottage near the base of the towering wall that held back fifteen billion gallons of water – water that relentlessly pushed forward in its quest to continually move downstream to the ocean. And in his nightmare, the dam would always break, sending a mountain of water, one hundred feet high, crashing down on the small cottage. Harnischfeger would then awaken in such a sweat that he would often wonder if he had, in some way, gotten drenched but managed to survive the disaster. His concern regarding his family's safety became so acute that the damkeeper constructed a crude set of steps up the west side of the canyon, near the cottage, as an escape route in the event something happened to the dam and sufficient warning could be given to allow their escape. It was not the most efficient safety precaution, but the escape route did offer him at least a modicum of comfort.

Harnischfeger could not admit to himself or to anyone else that he had any fear of the dam. He did, however, regard himself as a cautious man, and it was his duty to report any irregularities, such as seepage, etc., to the higher-ups. And it was seepage from the dam that prompted him to report the matter to the main office in Los Angeles that morning. To his distress, though, he was told that the big man himself, William Mulholland, would be driving out to inspect the dam personally.

As the dam keeper paced nervously atop the rampart, he frequently gazed southward, along the upper side of the canyon's west wall, where the roughly graded dirt road ran along the contours of the canyon. It was the primary route to the dam, and the road that Mulholland would travel to meet him.

Then, shortly after 10:30 A.M., the knot in the pit of the damkeeper's stomach tightened as he saw the unmistakable water company's executive vehicle lumbering slowly around the curves of the narrow, bumpy, dusty canyon road.

A moment later the big car, of the Packard vintage, pulled to the left side of the road and parked a dozen feet in front of the dam's west wing. The driver stepped out and opened the left rear door and waited for the occupant to emerge. The right rear door opened from within, and Harnischfeger recognized Harvey Van Norman getting out of the car. The sight of Van Norman, Mulholland's right-hand-man, brought a momentary sigh of relief to the damkeeper. Van Norman had a reputation for being an easy-going person with a friendly disposition – someone who would not jump down a man's throat at the least indiscretion.

But the moment of relief faded when the damkeeper saw the Chief slowly step out of the left passenger's side and walk around the car. At 72 years of age Mulholland walked with a slight stoop to his shoulders. His drooping mustache hid much of his facial expression, and if one were not accustomed to his dry sense of humor, that person might be left with the opinion that Mulholland was always in a bad mood. Harnischfeger was one such person. To say that the Chief intimidated him would be an understatement. To say that the mere presence of the Chief frightened the damkeeper into a state of almost complete immobility would be more accurate.

To Tony Harnischfeger, as well as to most of the lower-level employees of the water company, William Mulholland was larger than life. He was a giant. His feats in bringing water to an otherwise dry metropolis over the past quarter of a century had made him the most famous engineer in California, if not the entire United States. The people of Los Angeles, for the most part, loved him, while the folks up in the Owens Valley area hated him. But love him or hate him, most of the country stood in awe of William Mulholland's accomplishments.

Harnischfeger's feelings were a jumbled mess. Part of him resented the man. Part of him looked upon the Chief in wonder. The dam keeper tended to say critical things behind Mulholland's back that he would never say to his face. He knew that it was a cowardly way to be, and perhaps that was the reason for the resentment. At this moment, though, what Tony felt was fear of the man who was now approaching him atop the rampart.

"Mr. Harnischfeger," Mulholland inquired when he was within five feet of the damkeeper.

"Yes sir," Tony replied meekly.

"I believe you've met the Assistant Chief, Harvey Van Norman," Mulholland said, indicating the man standing to his right.

"Yes sir," Tony replied again.

Van Norman smiled warmly and nodded to the damkeeper. "Morning, Tony."

"Morning, sir."

"It is my understanding, Mr. Harnischfeger," Mulholland resumed, "that you detected muddy water flowing from a leak in the dam. Is that correct?"

"Yes sir, that's correct."

Mulholland's face remained expressionless, but within him a growing tension began to swell. Minor leaks in a dam were quite common, and usually presented no concerns as to the structural integrity of the dam, provided the water flowing from the leak was clear. If, however, the water was muddy, it could spell disaster. In all probability it would mean that foundation material was being eroded away from beneath the giant structure. Because the reservoir was full, it would be only a matter of time before the water pressure against the dam would cause the structure to collapse.

"Perhaps you could show us this leak and point out any other concerns you may have about the dam." Mulholland spoke in a calm voice. He had no intention of revealing his deep concerns about the leak to the damkeeper, for he was aware of Harnischfeger's loose tongue, and before he departed, the Chief was determined to discuss that matter with him.

"Yes, sir, I can do that," Tony said.

For the next two hours the three men inspected every foot of the structure's exposed area, beginning on the east side. Evidence of seepage was found in various places, but the seepage created nothing more than a minuscule trickle of clear water that dripped down the face of the dam. It was nothing to be concerned about.

Mulholland's driver, meanwhile, removed a camera from the car and descended the west bank of the canyon, where he began taking snapshots of the massive structure. He had obviously been directed to do so by the Chief prior to their arrival at the dam. The chauffeur then ascended the east bank and took shots from that angle before moving farther north to get a shot across the water, facing west by southwest. The photo took in the entire expanse of the dam, showing the three men standing together about midway along the rampart. The water in the foreground was at the top of the spillway. Little did the driver realize that, in the not-too-distant future, these photographs would become historic.

When the trio moved to the west side of the structure, where the leak that had caused all the concern was, Van Norman, who was more than two decades younger than the

Chief, descended the steep hillside adjacent to the site of the leak for a closer inspection. When he arrived at the precise spot where the water exited the dam he studied the escaping water keenly and was relieved to see that the water was quite clear. There was not a trace of material in suspension leaking from the dam.

As Van Norman carefully descended the hill, he followed the course of the stream that carried the leaking water. The stream flowed across the old construction road that had been used at the time the dam was being built, then down the hillside, where it picked up dirt that had been dumped during construction. It was at this point that the clear water became muddy. Van Norman reported his findings to the Chief and both men breathed heavy sighs of relief.

By this time the chauffeur had completed his picture-taking and had returned to the car. Mulholland suggested that Van Norman join the chauffeur, and he would be with them momentarily, for he had a few final suggestions to give to the damkeeper. Van Norman gave the Chief a knowing look then glanced uncomfortably at Harnischfeger.

"Be seeing you, Tony."

"Be seeing you, too, Mr. Van Norman," Tony replied, a note of nervous anticipation in his voice.

When they were alone Mulholland, standing no more than three feet in front of Harnischfeger, stared, unblinking, into the eyes of his subordinate. After what seemed an eternity to the damkeeper the Chief finally spoke.

"I've been hearing some rather disturbing stories about you, Mr. Harnischfeger."

"Wha ... what kind of stories, sir?"

"Oh, I think you know, Mr. Harnischfeger. For one thing, it has come to my attention that you have been allowing friends to have fishing parties out there on the reservoir, as if it were your own private lake." He waited a moment to see if Harnischfeger was going to reply. When he did not, Mulholland continued, "You know, of course, there is a strict policy against allowing anyone on the lake. The reason for that is quite clear. In the event of an accident, such as a drowning, the Los Angeles Water Company is liable – especially if an employee of the company invited them out onto the lake. I never want to hear of that again, is that clear?"

"Yes sir," Harnischfeger replied. Inwardly he felt a bit of relief, for the last sentence in the Old Man's tirade inferred that he would not be fired.

"Now I need to address a matter that, to me, is even more serious than allowing people onto the lake, and it has to do with your loose tongue."

"Why, I haven't ..." Harnischfeger began, but stopped when Mulholland held up his hand angrily in front of the damkeeper's face.

"Don't!" The Chief's face reddened, and his frown deepened behind the drooping mustache. "Don't anger me any more than I am already by some feeble attempt at denial. I know for a fact that you have been spreading gossip about the dam being unsafe. You visit friends and, before you leave you make remarks such as, 'I'll see you next week, that is, if the dam doesn't break in the meantime.' When your friends ask if they can fish in the lake, you reply, 'Sure, if the lake is still here when you come to fish.' Don't ask me how I know this. I have my sources."

Harnischfeger stared at his superior in disbelief – not because the allegations were untrue, but because the Old Man was aware of them. How could he know?

"For as long as large dams have been built throughout the world," Mulholland continued, "they have created a sense of insecurity among the residents who live downstream from them. This is natural, at least until the dam has been there for a while and the residents come to trust in its safety. But this dam is only two years old. People have not had time to get adjusted to it yet. It takes time. But when the damkeeper himself is constantly berating the dam, how are the residents expected to react? It is your responsibility to build that trust; not tear it down."

"Yes sir," Harnischfeger replied weakly, sensing a need to make some kind of response.

Mulholland went on, as if the damkeeper had not spoken. "And now I'm going to issue you a warning, Mr. Harnischfeger. If I ever hear of another occasion where you have badmouthed this dam, you will be fired immediately."

A long pause followed as Mulholland stared directly into the damkeeper's eyes. Harnischfeger wanted desperately to drop his eyes and stare at his feet, or at the Chief's feet – anywhere but into the Old Man's eyes.

"Yes sir." With that, Mulholland turned and walked slowly back to the car.

The driver, meantime, had turned the vehicle around and was facing down the canyon. As soon as the Chief was seated the car began rolling down the rough road. Mulholland leaned his head back on the seat and closed his eyes. A moment later he softly chuckled.

Van Norman looked at his superior and grinned. "I take it your conversation went well?"

"It was a bit one-sided, but, yes, I believe it went well." He chuckled again. "I don't think we will have any more problems with Tony."

A long, silent moment passed; then Van Norman's grin faded. "I did see something back there, Boss, that we're going to have to fix real soon."

Mulholland lifted his head from the backrest. He was suddenly all business again. "What is it, Van?"

"When I discovered that the water leaking from the dam was clear and I followed it down to where it became muddy, I noticed something else. I didn't want to say anything to you then, in front of Tony, because I knew there was nothing we could do immediately to fix the problem."

"What was it?"

"The water coming from the leak was not flowing in a slow, steady stream. There were frequent spurts shooting out. The concern, of course, is that the enormous pressure of the water against the wall of the structure may be causing the leak to slowly widen."

Mulholland thought for a moment. "This does present a problem. In order to repair the leak, it will be necessary to lower the water level. The reservoir is now full. It will take weeks to lower it to a level that will allow workmen to repair the leak." The Chief leaned his head back on the headrest and closed his eyes. Breathing a deep sigh, he added, "Oh, well. There's nothing to be done about it now. Let's go back to the office. In the next few days, we'll address the matter with staff. Perhaps someone will come up with a quicker solution than dropping the water level."

The car lumbered down the canyon road toward Los Angeles. Unknown to the two engineers, the vehicle was taking William Mulholland and Harvey Van Norman from their final visit to St. Francis Dam.

I:
MULHOLLAND
1877-1904

1

YOU DON'T KNOW ME. Never heard of me. My name's not important to this story so there's no need for me to introduce myself. What's important is that I knew Bill Mulholland inside and out, from the day he and his brother first rode into Los Angeles back in the late 1800s, all the way to the end of this story, more than half a century later.

You might have noticed that I referred to him as Bill. Actually, he was known by many names. When he was young some of his relatives called him Willie; others referred to him as Will, or William. After he became an important man in the water company he was known as Chief, or Boss. Those in the lower ranks – and out of the Chief's hearing – referred to him as the Old Man. Over the years Bill made a lot of enemies, and they also had a lot of names for him that I won't mention here. But as for me, I always just called him Bill.

What you are about to read you can take to the bank. Either I witnessed it myself or I learned of it from a reliable source shortly after the event in question. You might say that, for more than fifty years, where Bill Mulholland was concerned, I was the proverbial fly on the wall.

IT WAS A DRY, dusty January day in 1877 when 21-year-old William Mulholland and his younger brother, Hugh, rode into Los Angeles. Bill was not impressed by what he saw as he took in the surroundings from astride his horse. He saw no beauty in this dry, colorless pueblo that boasted a population of 9,000 souls.

The two brothers had entered the town from the north, and as they slowly rode south on the dirt road that was identified as Main Street by a crude sign they had noticed several yards behind them, they passed several adobe dwellings that seemed to emphasize the dryness and filth of the dusty ground on which they were erected. Between the drab gray houses were thatched coverings supported by an eight-foot pole in each corner. Under the coverings were several Mexicans – men, women and children. They all seemed to be taking naps – in the middle of the afternoon! No one was working!

There were also wooden structures, none of which had ever been painted, their surfaces long since bleached bone dry by the relentless rays of the sun. These, too, appeared to be private residences, but there was no one around.

The Mulholland brothers then rode past the Pico House on their left. The only building in the area made of red brick, it was, without a doubt, the most elegant hotel in the immediate vicinity. The structure stood out like a single rose placed upon a colorless pile of sand and debris. There were other hotels within a few blocks of one another, such as the United States and St. Elmo Hotels, but none as classy as the Pico House.

Less than half a block past and on the opposite side of the street from the Pico House the Mulhollands rode past a horse stable. It would be an understatement to say that it was poorly maintained. The foul stench that emanated from the stable, the ground of which overflowed onto the roadway with horse dung, was overwhelming. And the large flies that buzzed the vicinity of the establishment were a nuisance to any man or animal that had the misfortune to pass by the disgusting waste.

Continuing south, the brothers had just managed to ride a short distance beyond the range of the corral's offensive odor and began to breathe fresh, clean air when they found themselves adjacent to the main entrance of the St. Elmo Hotel. Both Mulhollands suddenly reined their mounts at the same time. But it was not the hotel that brought them to a halt. One door south was a saloon with a sign in the window advertising nickel beer and free sandwiches. Both of the brothers were hungry after their long ride, and the sign's offering was too tempting to pass up. Tying their horses in front of the saloon, they pushed through the batwing doors and proceeded to the end of the bar, where stacks of beef, ham, pork and cheese, along with pickles and loaves of bread, awaited them.

I would like to point out that I happened to be in the saloon sitting alone at a table in a corner nursing a mug of beer when the Mulholland brothers entered the establishment and was therefore a witness to everything that was said at that time.

When the young men entered I could tell at a glance they were related. Both were a bit taller than average. Each had a dark, thick, wavy mop of hair. Their facial structures were similar, with eyes and mouths that hinted at a no-nonsense nature about them.

As Bill and Hugh hungrily stacked meat and cheese onto slices of bread, the bartender, a middle-aged man with an enormous handlebar mustache, approached and said, "Boys, you're gonna have to order a drink if you wanna eat the grub."

"Yes sir," replied the elder Mulholland. "We'll have beer."

The bartender withdrew then returned a moment later with two mugs of cold beer, the foam flowing over the sides. Each with a beer in one hand and a plate full of sandwiches in the other, the two young men found a table near the window at the front of the saloon.

For the next five minutes they both ate ravenously, neither of them saying a word. It had been several days since either had eaten a full meal. They had departed San Francisco a week earlier with ten dollars and some change between them and a sack of biscuits and some beef jerky. In the San Joaquin Valley, the brothers had stopped at a farm and were treated well. That was the last decent meal they had eaten until now.

It was mid-afternoon and there were only a few patrons in the saloon. One man, standing at the bar, had been watching the two brothers ever since they first entered the establishment. Bill made a mental note of the man's apparent interest in them, but he chose to ignore it for the moment.

"Now that we've made it to Los Angeles," Hugh began, "where do we go from here?"

"Our next step is to locate Aunt Catherine," Bill said. After a pause, he added, "That is, if she and our cousins made it this far."

Having finished his beer, the man at the bar set his mug on the counter and moved to the table where the Mulhollands were sitting. He was a handsome man who appeared to be in his early thirties and was attired in a neat dark suit. He sported a full mustache and goatee, the two of which seemed to meet at the mouth. It was a solid mass of whiskers, three inches wide, from just beneath his nose to two inches below his chin and seemed to serve no purpose but to try to hide his otherwise youthful appearance.

"You boys just arrive in Los Angeles?" he asked.

"Yes sir, we did," Bill replied, then added, "Why do you want to know?"

The man opened the left lapel of his coat to reveal the badge of a deputy sheriff pinned to his shirt. He smiled and said, "Let's just say it's my job to know." He motioned to a vacant chair. "May I?"

"Help yourself," Bill said.

As he seated himself the man took off his hat and placed it on the table. "My name is Henry Mitchell. I'm the undersheriff of the county."

"What's an undersheriff?" Hugh wanted to know.

"The undersheriff is the number two law enforcement officer in Los Angeles County. Second only to the sheriff."

"My name's William Mulholland, and this is my brother, Hugh."

After the brothers shook hands with the undersheriff, Mitchell asked, "And what do you think of our fair city?"

"From what we've seen so far, not much," Bill replied. "We just passed some Mexican houses when we rode in and everyone was outside, under some kind of veranda or something, and they were all sound asleep – in the middle of the day! Doesn't anybody work in this town?"

Mitchell offered a patient smile. "The reason they aren't working is because this is the hottest part of the day. It's an old Mexican custom, and for my part, a very wise custom." After a pause, he continued, "You see, these people come from a hot, dry climate, and they learned a long time ago to adapt to the climate by working with it. So, they get up very early in the morning to begin their work day. Then, when the day is at its hottest point, they take a rest for a few hours. This is known as a *siesta*. Later in the afternoon, when it cools off, they resume their work, and will continue into the evening hours.

Mexican families often do not have their evening meals until late at night, perhaps ten p.m."

"But this is January, sir," Bill countered. "While it's not as cold as other parts of the country, the weather now seems to be fairly mild – certainly not too hot to work."

The undersheriff breathed a patient sigh, then spoke in a slightly softer tone. "Be that as it may, the siesta is a year-round custom. The Mexicans in our community are far from lazy. Quite the contrary. They are very hard workers."

Both brothers were quiet for a moment. Bill realized that he had misspoken, and he was momentarily embarrassed. He did not like this awkward feeling. It didn't sit well with him. He wanted very much to change the subject. Then his eyes lit up as a thought occurred to him. "You're right, sir, I prejudged those folks, but that wasn't the only thing that rubbed us raw as we rode into town. For instance, what about the smell around here?"

"Come again?" Mitchell asked.

"We passed a corral back there that stunk up the whole block. How can people put up with such an awful stench?"

Mitchell chuckled. "You must mean old Joshua Hewitt's stable. Yes, you're right. In fact, the Pico House has filed a complaint with the city, requesting that Mr. Hewitt's corral either be cleaned up or shut down completely. It seems that the foul odor has made its way into every room in the hotel."

"How long has it been like that?" Bill wanted to know.

"Several months now, I guess."

"Several months! Why does it take so long to get the matter settled?"

Mitchell shrugged his shoulders and shook his head. "I don't know. Wheels of justice, I guess."

An awkward silence followed, then Mitchell asked, "Could I buy you fellows another round?"

Both brothers perked up and smiled. "Sure. We'd be obliged," Bill said.

After the beers were delivered to the table, the undersheriff asked, "So, what other complaints do you have about our city?"

Bill could not help but grin. "We just barely got into town. Isn't what we said enough?"

Mitchell smiled. Bill decided he liked the undersheriff. There was a friendliness about him that was real, and his smile also came across as genuine.

Before speaking, Mitchell's smile faded. "Actually, I can think of at least three things about our town that should cause you some serious concern ... that is, if you fellows are planning to settle here."

"Oh? And what might those things be?" Bill asked.

"For one thing, Los Angeles is in the middle of a depression. Secondly, I don't know if you noticed it or not, but we are also experiencing a drought. And finally, we are in the latter stages of a smallpox epidemic."

The brothers looked at one another. "Smallpox!" they both repeated.

Mitchell saw the concern on both their faces and said, "Don't worry too much about the smallpox. From what I'm told it is on its way out. Besides, most of the ones who came down with it were Mexicans and Chinese. There weren't a great number of whites who caught it." When neither of the brothers spoke, he added, "The ones who have caught it, at least the Mexicans and Chinese, have been quarantined."

"Where are they being held?" Bill asked.

"A few miles northwest of here – a place called Chavez Ravine."

A wry smile appeared on Bill's face as he shook his head slowly.

"What is it?" Mitchell asked. "What's wrong?"

"Well, it's just that the reason we came to Los Angeles was to escape a sickness back east."

"Smallpox?"

"No. Tuberculosis. A few years ago, when Hugh and I came over to America from Ireland, our Uncle Richard and Aunt Catherine Deakers took us into their home in Pittsburgh – Uncle Richard is our departed mother's brother – and we worked in their dry goods store. They are wonderful people.

"Well, about two years ago tuberculosis came upon the family, and eventually two of our cousins – Uncle Richard and Aunt Catherine had eight children – died of the disease. It was then that the decision was made to come west to a drier climate. Aunt Catherine has a brother who lives out here somewhere and he said the climate is dry and suited for those with lung problems." After a slight shrug and a sigh, Bill concluded, "So here we are."

"How did you get separated from the Deakers?"

"Ah, and that's another story, " Hugh put in.

"Why don't you tell it?" Bill urged.

"No, Willie. You're the talker. You go ahead and tell it."

"Well, Uncle Richard had to stay behind to close out the dry goods business and sell the house, and such. But Aunt Catherine and our six remaining cousins took passage on a large three-deck passenger ship out of New York. Hugh and I did not have enough money to pay our fare, but we assured Aunt Catherine that we would find a way to Los Angeles and would meet them here." Bill grinned. "Actually, Hugh and I started out aboard the same ship as the Deakers ... as stowaways."

Mitchell smiled, but said nothing, allowing Bill to continue uninterrupted.

"Eventually we were caught, and when the ship reached the port at Colon, in Panama, we were kicked off. Having no money for train fare across the Isthmus, we had to walk the forty-seven miles through some pretty thick jungle. When we arrived in Balboa, on the Pacific side, Hugh and I signed on to a Peruvian man-of-war that was headed for Acapulco. From there we were lucky enough to catch a northbound ship headed for San Francisco. In San Francisco, we bought two horses and food with money earned on the Peruvian ship. That left us with ten dollars and some change, which is all we have with us right now."

A silence fell over the trio when Bill finished speaking. After a moment Mitchell said, "I'm curious, just how old are you two? You can't be much older than nineteen or twenty, and yet you seem to have crammed so much experience into such a short period of time in your lives."

"Well, Hugh here is twenty, and I'm twenty-one. I'll be twenty-two in September." Following another brief pause, he continued, "You see, I ran away from our home in Dublin when I was fourteen and became a merchant seaman. A year later I joined the British Merchant Marine. By the time I was sixteen I had crossed the Atlantic half a dozen times, between England, Ireland, the Bahamas and America. After a while I got tired and decided to leave the sea, so one day I just walked off the ship and didn't return. Thankfully, we were in an American port at the time.

"I moved about quite a bit, doing odd jobs, then I ran into Hugh. Seems our father enrolled him in the British Navy right after Hugh turned fifteen. When his ship came into port here in America, Hugh decided that he had had enough of the Brits, so he jumped ship. We've been together ever since."

"So, what is your next move?"

"Our next move is to try and find the whereabouts of our aunt Catherine." Bill stared at the undersheriff for a long moment, then a thought occurred to him. "Say, Mr. Mitchell, as the undersheriff you must know a lot of important people around here – perhaps someone who deals in house rentals and the like, who might have come across our aunt. Do you think you might be able to help us locate her?"

Undersheriff Mitchell thought for a minute before replying, "I'm sure I know a few people who may be able to locate the Deakers family – that is, if they made it to Los Angeles." He motioned the bartender over, and when the man with the handlebar mustache arrived Mitchell said, "Homer, these two gentlemen are my guests. I am going to ask them to remain here until I return. Let them have whatever they want and charge it to me. I'll be back shortly."

"Yes sir," the bartender said before withdrawing.

"Is this all right with you fellows?" Mitchell asked. "I shouldn't be more than an hour or so. Hopefully, when I get back I will have the information you need on your kinfolks."

"Yes sir, this will be fine," Bill said, with Hugh nodding in the affirmative.

Mitchell arose and headed for the door. Bill called after him and the undersheriff turned. "Mr. Mitchell, we sure appreciate what you're doing. It means a lot to us."

Mitchell smiled and nodded to the brothers, then walked out of the saloon.

2

IT WAS ALMOST two hours later when Mitchell returned to the saloon. He was accompanied by a man who appeared to be a year or so older than the undersheriff. The man was a few inches shorter than Mitchell, and not as formally dressed. The star-shaped badge of a deputy sheriff was pinned to his shirt just above the left breast pocket.

Mitchell approached the Mulholland brothers with a smile. "Good news, gentlemen," he said as he moved to their table.

The brothers both stood as the undersheriff arrived with his companion. "You located our aunt?" Bill asked.

"Yes, we did." Mitchell paused then added, "At least I'm ninety-five percent sure we've located the right Deakers."

Bill and Hugh exchanged glances. When neither of them spoke, Mitchell continued, "I believe you mentioned that your aunt was accompanied by six children."

"That's right."

Mitchell's smile faded and he cleared his throat. "Well, we've located a Catherine Deakers, having recently arrived in Los Angeles with her *four* children, now living in a small cottage on Pico, a few miles from here."

Bill glanced at his brother, who stared disbelievingly at the undersheriff. "Four children? Not six?"

Mitchell nodded solemnly.

"Is it possible your source could be wrong about the number of children that were with Catherine Deakers?" Bill asked.

Mitchell took a deep breath then exhaled it in a long, weary sigh. "I suppose anything is possible, William." After a pause he added, "But don't get your hopes up. My source was quite certain of his findings."

Following a long moment of awkward silence, Henry Mitchell said, "Please forgive my rudeness, gentlemen, but I failed to introduce you to Deputy Jim Boyer. Jim, this is William and Hugh Mulholland." Addressing the Mulhollands he said, "I've asked Jim, here, to escort you fellows over to your aunt's house down on Pico. It's only a couple miles from here, but I thought having someone to show you the way would be easier than drawing a map or giving directions."

The brothers looked at Deputy Boyer and he smiled and nodded. Bill and Hugh returned the nod.

"As a matter of fact," Mitchell continued, "if you fellows want to arrive at your aunt's house before dark, you should leave now. Sundown comes pretty early this time of year."

Ten minutes later the Mulholland brothers, along with Deputy Boyer, were astride their horses in front of the saloon.

"Thanks for everything, Mr. Mitchell," Bill said, addressing the undersheriff, who was standing on the boardwalk in front of them.

"Same here," Hugh added. "If there's anything we can do for you, just let us know."

"Well, it's funny you should mention that, Hugh," Mitchell said with a grin. "There might be something you can do – that is, if you boys decide to stick around and settle here."

"Name it."

"Well, I don't want to sound too premature, but, if our current sheriff, good man that he is, chooses not to run for another term, I aim to run for the office myself." He grabbed the lapels of his coat politician-style and moved up and down on the balls of his feet. "Well, now, I would consider it a great favor if you could see your way to vote for me this coming fall."

Both brothers returned the grin, then Bill replied, "I'll tell you what, sir. I honestly can't tell you where we will be this coming fall, but if we are in Los Angeles you can count on my vote, that's for certain."

"The same goes for me," Hugh added.

Mitchell ceased his politician antics and became serious. "You fellows have a safe trip, and my prayers go out to the Deakers family."

The brothers nodded, then the three horsemen turned their mounts southward and rode down Main Street.

Deputy Jim Boyer and I had been close friends for years. In fact, I stood up for him at his wedding. And it was from him that I learned everything there was to know about the trip to the Deakers' house.

SOUTH OF TOWN looked much like it did on the north side. Orange groves graced much of the landscape, with frequent outcroppings of desert growth. Adobe dwellings appeared here and there along the roadside, and to a lesser extent, the riders passed occasional wood-framed structures. The leaves on the orange trees, though still green, were turned inward, a sure sign of the drought that Los Angeles was experiencing.

The road turned in a southwesterly direction south of the more densely populated part of town. After riding along in silence for several minutes, Deputy Boyer asked, "You boys planning on settling down hereabouts?"

"We're not sure yet," Bill answered. "We thought we'd look around and see what kind of work might be available to us." Silently, he was gradually reaching the conclusion that he was not impressed with anything he had seen so far.

"I know we've been going through some pretty rough times lately," Boyer said, "and Los Angeles ain't much to look at right now, but I do believe that this place has a lot to offer." He paused and looked around. "Yes sir, some day this place is gonna grow."

"What makes you so sure?" Bill wanted to know.

"Well, because we got the resources to make something big of this place."

"What kind of resources?"

"For one thing, we got two seaports: one in Santa Monica and one in San Pedro. And recently the Southern Pacific Railroad completed laying tracks all the way from San Francisco to Los Angeles, meaning that we are now connected by rail to the rest of the country. And third, just look around you, at all the citrus groves. They're all over the place, for miles around. We could be the biggest producer of citrus crops in the country." The deputy then frowned and heaved an audible sigh. "That is, if we had one other natural resource."

"And what might that be?" Bill asked.

"Water." He motioned with his thumb back toward town. "There's a river that runs along the east side of town. It's pretty shallow as rivers go, but it provides enough water for the town folk. But if we continue to grow, it will not support us." He paused again then added, "Even now it doesn't provide enough irrigation for the trees around here."

Mulholland offered a wry smile. "I would say water is a rather significant natural resource to be considered. I admire your hope for the growth of the town, but how do you propose to solve the water problem?"

Deputy Boyer thought for a moment then shrugged his shoulders. "I don't know, Mr. Mulholland. I'll save that for someone to come along who's a lot smarter than I am. In the meantime, I'll just continue to hope."

Several minutes later Deputy Boyer brought his horse to a stop in the middle of what appeared to be a wide intersection of three roads. The southwest-bound road on which they had been traveling had met a wide west-bound road, as well as a third road heading south.

When the brothers reined up alongside the deputy, he explained, "Off to the west is the stage route that goes out to the Pacific Ocean at Santa Monica. To the south is the stage route that runs down to San Pedro. The stages come this far from the ports then follow the road we've been on the rest of the way into town. The main stop in town is the St. Charles Hotel, formerly the Bella Union Hotel. It ain't much now, but when it was the Bella Union, there was no place like it around." After a brief pause, he added, "I guess the stages ain't found any reason to change locations, so they still stop there."

When the brothers offered no comment, Boyer resumed, "We'll go south on the San Pedro stage road for a short ways then turn west on the Pico road. That's the road your aunt lives on. It shouldn't be too much longer."

Shortly after resuming their journey, Hugh asked, "Do you think Mr. Mitchell was serious about running for sheriff, or was he just kidding us?"

"Oh, he was serious, all right," Boyer said. "Alexander – he's our current sheriff – has made no secret of the fact that he ain't all that interested in running for another term, and it's fairly certain that Henry Mitchell is the man to replace him."

"Why do you say he's the man to replace the current sheriff?"

"Well, he's well-liked around the county. Most of the former sheriffs support him, including Sheriff Alexander. He's proven that he can do the job, and he's one of the smartest men around." The deputy looked at the brothers. "Did he happen to mention to either of you that he was a lawyer?"

"A lawyer?" Bill asked. "No."

"Well, if he's a lawyer, why would he want to run for sheriff?" Hugh wanted to know. "Why don't he just practice law?"

Boyer grinned. "He tried that when he first hung out his shingle." He chuckled before continuing. "He was in his mid-twenties when he began practicing law, but he had such a youthful appearance no one seemed to take him serious as a lawyer. That's why he grew that awful looking mustache and goatee – to make him look older. In the meantime, he not only took on other jobs to support hisself, such as deputy sheriff, but he also became a notary public and a volunteer fireman. He's now known all over the county, and now has a fairly good law practice, but I guess sheriffin' has sort of gotten in his blood."

"He does seem friendly enough," Bill said.

"And he sure dresses nice," Hugh added.

"Well, don't let them fancy duds fool you. Henry Mitchell is as tough a lawman as you'll find anywhere. Why, just a couple years ago, when Billy Rowland was sheriff, he and Mitchell and a few other deputies went out and captured Tiburcio Vasquez and brought him in for trial. Him and his gang was holed up in a shack owned by a fellow known as Greek George. There was a big shoot-out and most of the gang got away, but not Vasquez. He was wounded in the arm, but he survived – that is, he lived long enough to be hung."

The Mulhollands exchanged glances before Hugh said, "Tiburcio Vasquez? I never heard of him."

The expression on the deputy's face was one of disbelief. "What?" he asked as he stared from one brother to the other.

The brothers both shrugged their shoulders then Bill spoke. "Deputy Boyer, we just got into town this afternoon, and only recently arrived in California from Pennsylvania." He paused before adding, almost apologetically, "I don't think anyone back east has ever heard of Tiburcio Vasquez."

About this time the riders arrived at the Pico road, and they turned west, but Boyer was too vexed to make any comment about the change of direction. "Well, let me just educate you boys on Mr. Vasquez. This man was the most despicable, meanest, murdering, thievingest outlaw that ever roamed this part of the country. Every lawman south of San Francisco was looking for him. Tiburcio Vasquez was known to shoot down man, woman or child – Chinese, Mexican or white – made no difference to him. He was as slippery as they come. But he was finally caught, and it took the likes of Billy Rowland and Henry Mitchell to do it."

For the next several minutes the three men rode in silence. Bill was caught up in thoughts of sheriffs' posses and outlaw bands and shootouts. There was an excitement about it that seemed to awaken a call for adventure that was in his Irish blood. There was so much life and energy in this land, and where there was life and energy there was adventure, and where there was adventure, there would be challenge. As he pondered this, he began to realize that it was a challenge that he longed for, perhaps even more than the adventure that would inevitably accompany the challenge.

The sun was a big orange ball dropping slowly somewhere behind the horizon of the Pacific Ocean, the coast of which was twenty miles west of where they now rode, when Deputy Boyer reined his horse in front of a modest wood framed house on the south side of the dirt road. It was more of a cottage than a house, and had once been whitewashed, but now had a grayish appearance. Between the road and the small front yard was a sun-bleached picket fence. The grass, what there was of it, was brown, as it was everywhere in the area.

"Well," Boyer said, "according to my directions, this is where your aunt lives. Would either of you boys like to go up to the porch and make sure these folks are your kin?"

Without comment both brothers alit from their mounts and proceeded to the front of the house. Hugh was in the lead, and when he arrived at the door he knocked without hesitating. A moment later a girl in her early teens opened the door. She took one look and her eyes widened, but she said nothing.

Hugh smiled and said, "Hi, Ella!"

Ella turned and ran toward one of the back rooms. "Mama! Mama!" she shouted. "Hugh and Willie are here!"

Hugh looked at Bill and grinned broadly. A moment later their Aunt Catherine appeared at the door. She was a woman of medium height and weight. As she approached, she wiped her hands on her apron. "Mary, mother of God!" she exclaimed. "You made it!"

3

I DIDN'T HEAR MUCH about either of the Mulholland brothers over the next month or so, but reliable sources did inform me that, upon arriving at their Aunt Catherine's house, they learned the sad news that two more of her children, after having overcome pneumonia symptoms, each contracted typhoid and died aboard ship.

Rumor also had it that both Bill and Hugh were unhappy with Los Angeles. Try as they might, neither was able to find any kind of decent employment. After a few months of disappointment, Bill decided to go down to San Pedro and try to sign on to a ship. With his seamanship experience he figured he would have little trouble finding one. Having no money to take the stage, he set about walking the twenty miles or more to the harbor.

Then fate stepped into his life.

He had been walking two hours or so when he came upon a man digging a well several yards off the side of the road. Out of curiosity Bill stopped and watched the man work. One thing led to another, and the man offered him a job. Without giving it a second thought, Bill took it.

MANUEL DOMINGUEZ was the name of the man who hired him. The newly founded town of Compton had hired

Dominguez to hand drill a series of wells to serve the city's needs.

Mulholland was no stranger to hard work, and the salary Mr. Dominguez offered seemed fair. As he labored at the hand drill Bill slowly realized that it was not Los Angeles that he resented so much. It was the frustration he felt in being unable to find decent work.

The two men took turns at the drill, the bit of which descended deeper and deeper into the earth. When it reached the six-hundred-foot level it hit a tree. When the bit was recovered, Bill was fascinated to find pieces of wood attached to it. After cleaning the bit, they lowered it back into the hole. It passed through the tree and continued downward several more feet until it hit a bed of fossils. This was evidenced by the particles that adhered to the bit when it was returned to the surface.

Seldom had Bill been so captivated by anything in his life. In later years he recounted the incident by stating, "These things fired my curiosity. I wanted to know how those things got there and so I got hold of Joseph LeConte's book on the geology of this country. Right there I decided to become an engineer."

Well, it sounds nice, but it wasn't all that cut and dried. There was a tough road ahead of him, and at least one side trip to take, before Mr. William Mulholland could honestly call himself an engineer.

While Bill was gainfully employed, and over the months had managed to bring home more than a few paychecks to assist in his room and board, his brother, Hugh, had not been so fortunate. Occasionally he was able to find a day's labor here and there, but nothing that had any sense of permanence – nothing fulfilling. The more time passed the more Hugh's disenchantment with Los Angeles grew.

One of the current topics of conversation around town was the recent discovery of gold in the southwestern region of Arizona Territory. Several local residents of Los Angeles had even discussed joining in on the rush to strike it rich, yet very few seemed sufficiently motivated to make the journey. That is, until one day when Hugh approached Bill and told him of his plans to make the trip to Arizona. At first Bill was taken aback at such an idea, but the more he thought about it, the more attracted to this hare-brained scheme he became. Even if they didn't strike it rich, the mere adventure of it would make the trip worth the time invested in it. It took very little additional persuading on Hugh's part before Bill made up his mind to quit his job and join his sibling on the journey.

Soon the two brothers, each with more grit and adventure under their belts than most men twice their age, were aboard the eastbound stage, headed for the Arizona Territory. It was now late summer, and the long ride took them across some of the hottest deserts in the country. They rode in the coach, with a hot breeze blowing through the windows. At least the breeze moved the air and provided the only relief to the sweltering heat of the desert.

When, at last, they arrived in Ehrenberg, a bustling town northeast of Yuma, they found a town brimming with ranchers, cowboys and gold seekers walking the streets and filling the saloons and general stores. The prospecting equipment the Mulhollands would need sold at premium prices, so it was necessary for the brothers to find work to purchase the equipment.

They found employment working on the steamboats that carried people and cargo along the Colorado River, between Yuma and Ehrenberg. As they worked on the paddle wheelers, they often heard talk of Indian raids throughout the southern regions of the Territory. These raids were being carried out by the likes of Victorio and Geronimo. The very mention of these two Apache legends were enough to strike fear in the hearts of most newcomers, among whom were Bill and Hugh. Unlike Tiburcio Vasquez, these two names were certainly familiar to them, even back in Pennsylvania.

After earning enough for their supplies, including food and other staples, the brothers set out to find gold. They found a spot among several other prospectors who shared with them the dream of striking it rich, and the brothers began the laborious task of digging, searching for the illusive treasure. They were at it for only a short time when a unit of Army cavalry rode into Ehrenberg with a warning that Geronimo was seen in the area, raiding local ranches. Everyone should stay alert.

The stories they had heard back east about Geronimo and the Apaches were tales of horror – of scalping and butchering of men, women and children. This was not the sort of adventure the Mulholland brothers had in mind. The stagecoach ride across the desert and working on the paddle wheeler were adventure. Getting outfitted and digging for gold was an adventure. Getting butchered by savages was just plain suicide.

Having seen no sign of color in their brief digging efforts, the brothers decided that the threat of the dreaded Geronimo was sufficient cause for them to abandon their search for gold and return to civilization. When the next southbound stage for Yuma departed, the Mulholland brothers were among its passengers. From Yuma, Bill and Hugh rode a passenger train all the way to Los Angeles. Their short-lived adventure had come to an end.

4

IN SEPTEMBER 1877 Bill celebrated his 22nd birthday. Two months later elections were held in Los Angeles County and Henry Mitchell was elected Sheriff. Alexander, having decided not to run for re-election, announced his support of Mitchell.

The year came to an end and 1878 arrived with little change. The smallpox epidemic had been eradicated, but money and jobs were still in short supply, as was water.

Ever since returning to Los Angeles from Arizona it was quite clear that Hugh was not a happy man. He was restless. There was a drive within him to find his own way in the world. So, one day he just up and announced that he was leaving. Wasn't sure where he was going but would know when he got there. His family seemed to understand. I suppose it was something within them that they all shared. So, they said their farewells and Hugh departed.

Bill and Hugh would keep in touch and, on occasion, join one another in some joint venture that usually went nowhere. I believe this was Bill's attempt at lending a hand to his younger brother. As for this story there is little further mention of Hugh.

As for me, when he left Los Angeles, it was the last time I ever saw the younger Mulholland.

BILL'S DREAM OF BECOMING an engineer never left him, even during his and Hugh's adventure in Arizona. Now that he was back in Los Angeles, Bill was determined more than ever to see his dream come true. After scraping up enough money he ordered more books that would further his education in the field of civil engineering. It was also about this time, early in the year 1878, that he went to work for the water company. He was hired by Fred Eaton, the 22-year-old superintendent of the company. Eaton and Mulholland would become friends in the coming years.

Please forgive my constant interruptions, but I should mention something about the name of Bill's employer. During these early days in Los Angeles, when water was a huge political and financial issue, there were three – probably more – water interests fighting to gain control of the water rights throughout the region. A great deal of money was to be made by whoever ended up owning the water rights in Los Angeles. The municipal government was continually at odds with the private interests. It went back and forth. Though Bill would, during his early years, work for more than one company, he was, in effect, doing the same job. The water wars in the early days of Los Angeles are a story unto themselves, and volumes have been written about them, and though Bill Mulholland was caught up in much of it, that conflict is not relevant to this story. So, at least for his early years, his employer will simply be referred to as "the water company."

AS RIVERS GO, the Los Angeles River could never be counted among the great waterways of the world. Its origin was somewhere in the western foothills of the San Fernando

Valley, with waters coming in from the Tujunga Wash, some thirty miles northwest of the city's plaza. Except for extremely rare thunderstorms, when the banks of the river would almost overflow from a raging torrent of water rushing south in a deadly race to empty itself into the Pacific Ocean, the river could be described as little more than a glorified stream, seldom more than a foot deep, flowing along in a very slow current. The willows that grew along its banks created a peaceful setting, as well as a welcome shade from the summer sun. But more importantly, the Los Angeles River, as modest as the water flow was, provided the growing community with its life's blood; and without the river, there would never have been a Los Angeles.

In 1864, fourteen years before Bill went to work for the water company, a long flume was installed, extending out several feet beyond the banks of the Los Angeles River. At the end of the flume a huge water wheel was constructed, which lifted containers of water up to the flume where it flowed into a ditch. The ditch, in turn, carried the water to a reservoir near the city's plaza. It was here that Mulholland began his career with the water company.

He was hired on as a deputy *zanjero*, which is Spanish for one in charge of water distribution from the *zanja* (irrigation ditch). In later years Bill would say that his first job was that of ditch digger. In reality it was more than that. A *zanjero* actually maintained the ditches. Although digging in the ditch was part of his job, there was more to it than just digging. He kept weeds and debris out of it, including the carcasses of dead animals. It was his job to keep the ditch as clean and free flowing as possible, for it was the water source for the community. Occasionally there were water poachers; that is, people stealing water from the ditches, and it was the deputy *zanjero's* job to prevent such activity.

His salary was $1.50 a day, and he worked six days a week, with Sundays off. He was also provided with a small house to live in which was located near the river, within a short walk to his work site. Though he later referred to the structure as a shack, it was said as an endearment, for he treasured the two years that he spent living in the modest house that sat under the shade of a sycamore tree. This was also the first place that Bill could truly call a home of his own. In every other place he lived, he had been the guest of someone else.

After getting off work each evening Bill would go directly home, where he would clean himself up, fix a bite of supper, then go directly to his engineering studies. As the weeks turned into months, he managed to collect a sizeable number of books and treatises on engineering. His work in the water company was undoubtedly a factor in his attention being drawn more closely to hydraulic engineering. He was a voracious reader and studied well into the night. He now knew what he wanted, and it was only a matter of time before his dream would come to fruition.

His main food staple was canned salmon, along with various fresh vegetables and, perhaps, oatmeal for breakfast. The nine-dollar-a-week salary that he brought home was more than enough to make ends meet, and most of that money was spent on reading material.

It is hard to say exactly when Bill Mulholland decided to grow a mustache, but it was probably shortly after being hired by the water company. And, in time, the neatly trimmed dark brown horseshoe-shaped growth below his nose added a distinctive feature to the young man's handsome face.

Bill was a hard worker, and he took his job seriously. No matter how menial the task might appear to others,

Mulholland put his whole heart into it. As the months passed his body became lean and muscular.

ONE SUNDAY AFTERNOON in early fall Bill was in his yard, kneeling on the ground near the sycamore tree. In his hand was a tiny three-inch seedling that he had pulled from the side of the ditch he was widening the day before. He immediately recognized the seedling as an oak in its infancy and had placed it inside one of his empty salmon cans and filled the can with wet soil. And now he was in the process of planting it. It was his dream to be around some day to see the seedling grow into a sturdy oak. He gently placed it into a small hole that he had previously dug, then began filling it, careful not to damage the little seedling.

Bill was so engrossed in his work that he did not hear the horse move up behind him.

"Good afternoon, William," a voice said from atop the mount.

"What the hell!" Bill exclaimed as he stood and wheeled around. He was clearly startled.

He was about to lash out at the intruder but stopped short as he suddenly recognized the visitor.

"Sheriff Mitchell! You really gave me a start. I didn't hear you ride up."

The sheriff offered a gentle smile. He had not intended to cause such a reaction as this, and he regretted his rudeness. "I'm really sorry, William. I should have yelled out back a ways."

Having recovered from his momentary embarrassment, Bill said, "No harm done, Sheriff." After a pause he added, "How about getting down and visiting for a while?"

"What are you planting?" the sheriff asked before dismounting.

"It's an oak seedling I found near the ditch."

"May I offer you a suggestion?" the sheriff asked.

Bill shrugged. "Sure."

"You might want to consider planting it much farther from the sycamore." Nodding toward the sycamore, he added, "That sycamore is quite young, and has not reached its full size. In a few years it can reach as much as one hundred feet high, with its branches extending, perhaps, twenty-five feet from the trunk. It will overshadow your young oak."

"Thanks for letting me know," Bill replied as he glanced down at the site where he had just planted the seedling.

As Mitchell was alighting from his mount Bill said, "Why don't we go into the house. It's a bit cooler inside. I'll put a pot of coffee on, and we can get caught up on things."

"I'd like that," the sheriff said as he followed Mulholland into the ditch tender's modest home.

As they entered the wooden structure Mitchell noted that it was, indeed, cooler inside the house. He decided that the carpenters must have insulated it quite well when building it. Also, he observed that a screened window had been placed on each of the four sides of the building, enabling the house to capture a breeze from whatever direction it blew.

As Bill poured water into the coffee pot, followed by a generous portion of grounds, he fed the hot embers inside the stove that still glowed from his last meal, with additional wood, then set the pot atop the stove.

As Bill carried out this chore it gave the sheriff a chance to take in the surroundings. The interior of Mulholland's home was the very picture of a Spartan existence. Near the stove was a simple wooden table with two straight chairs, neither of which matched the other, nor did either match the table, though all three appeared to be clean and solid. In fact, the entire house was clean. In a corner was a single bed, barely large enough for Mulholland's larger-than-average frame. On the other side of the room, opposite the kitchen area, at least four shelves of books took up much of the wall space. In a corner was a desk, the top of which was graced with a kerosene lamp, a collection of pens and pencils, as well as a large writing tablet. Scattered about atop the desk were various tools such as rulers, protractors, and other calculating devices.

"You know, Sheriff," Bill began, his back to Mitchell as he stood in front of the stove preparing the coffee, "though we haven't spoken since that day I first met you and you helped Hugh and me locate our Aunt Catherine, I have been following newspaper accounts of your exploits. I even attended a speech you gave in front of the courthouse last April. But, of course, nothing can hold a candle to the gun battle you had with that Sotello character this past June. Why, that was front page news for several days running."

Mulholland was referring to Miguel Sotello, the last member of the Tiburcio Vasquez gang. The sheriff had gotten word that Sotello was hanging out in a bar in Verdugo Canyon. Anxious to close the book on the Vasquez matter for good, Mitchell obtained a superior court bench warrant for Sotello's arrest, then he and a deputy named Adolf Celis set out for Verdugo Canyon. As the two lawmen rode up to the bar Sotello spotted them and ran out the door, jumped on his horse and quickly galloped away. Mitchell and Celis spurred their own mounts and went after him. Sotello turned in his saddle and took a shot at his pursuers. Both lawmen returned fire as the chase wove through the canyon, the pursuers and the pursued exchanging fire. They had ridden hard for two miles when Sotello suddenly slumped in the saddle for a moment, then slid from the horse. He was mortally wounded. They took him into custody, and he died the following morning. The incident was indeed headline news for the next several days, for Sotello's death would be a final reminder of the violence that had been part of his era.

Following an awkward silence, Sheriff Mitchell said, "Well, I have to say it was a memorable experience. But I would be less than truthful if I didn't give at least half the credit for the way it turned out to Adolf Celis. As far as I'm concerned, there's no lawman in the world I'd rather have at my side than Deputy Celis. They don't come any better."

Mulholland looked over his shoulder and offered a knowing smile, then turned back to his coffee-making. Mitchell moved toward the bookshelves and began scanning the titles on the covers. Most of them pertained to subjects related to geology, mathematics, hydraulics, and engineering. There were some classic novels, several works of Shakespeare, as well as a few volumes of poetry. Henry Mitchell was intrigued by his friend's taste in reading.

Mulholland set two cups of steaming hot coffee on the table just as Mitchell turned from the bookshelves and moved toward the center of the room. After both men sat down Mitchell reached for the small container of cream which Bill had previously placed on the table. He then remarked, "I must say, William, I am quite impressed with your collection of books."

"Yes sir." Bill took a sip of coffee then leaned back in his chair.

"Since I saw you last, I've decided what I want to do with my life."

Before the sheriff could respond, Mulholland went on, "I've decided to become an engineer." He paused briefly then added, "Not just an engineer, but a hydraulic engineer."

"And what made you decide to become an engineer?"

The younger man took a long moment before answering as he seemed to gaze absently at the ceiling. When he spoke it was slowly, as if reflecting carefully. "I suppose the seed might have been planted the day Hugh and I first rode into town. You recall when you had Deputy Boyer escort us to our Aunt Catherine's house?"

The sheriff nodded but said nothing.

Bill resumed. "Well, on that ride Boyer got to talking about the wonderful potential for growth there was in Los Angeles. Two sea ports, a railroad, good weather and the prospects of a booming citrus industry. The only thing it lacked was a proper water supply. The water from local sources was sufficient for the time being, but as the population grows it will not suffice. And there will certainly not be enough to support a citrus industry." He paused as if reflecting on what he had just said, then added, "I recall putting an end to the conversation with the deputy by concluding there was nothing to be done about it. And yet, something about that conversation stuck in my head – like a puzzle, or maybe a riddle – that had an answer. All it needed was someone to figure it out."

"And that was it?' Mitchell asked.

"No. Well, that was part of it, but there was more." Bill then went on to relate the time he decided to walk down to San Pedro and try to hire on as a ship's crewman when he was hired by a well digger named Manuel Dominguez, and the fascinating discoveries found in the excavations that motivated him to study engineering. It was after he hired on as a ditch tender that he became interested in hydraulic engineering. The more he observed the water situation in Los Angeles and the more he delved into the world of engineering the more determined he became that a solution to the water problem was out there somewhere.

Sheriff Mitchell took a sip of the now luke-warm coffee and placed the mug on the table. He regarded his host for a moment then smiled, still unable to hide his youthful appearance behind the thick whiskers.

"William," he began, "you're not telling me anything I don't know already. Of course, I'm aware that your Aunt Catherine arrived safely in Los Angeles. Deputy Boyer informed me after returning from escorting you to their home. But I am also aware of the unfortunate loss of two of your cousins who died of typhoid aboard ship en route to Los Angeles. And that your Uncle Richard Deakers, who had stayed behind in Pittsburgh to close out his business, safely arrived in Los Angeles a few months ago and the Deakers family is doing quite well now."

Mulholland stared across the table at his guest but said nothing. His face was expressionless.

Mitchell continued, "I am also well aware that you went to work as a well digger for my good friend, Manuel Dominguez. Did Senor Dominguez happen to mention to you that he is the grandson of the original grantee to Rancho San Pedro? It was one of the largest land grants in this part of the country."

"Mister Dominguez made no mention of that," Mulholland replied. He spoke softly and continued to stare across the table at his guest.

"Senor Dominguez thinks very highly of you, William. He said that you impressed him as a very intelligent young man and believes that you will go far in the world. It was he who told me of your desire to study engineering."

Another long moment of silence passed before Mulholland spoke. "Why, Sheriff? Why have you taken so much trouble to look into what I've been up to? We only met that one time. I must admit that both Hugh and I took a liking to you, and we were both very grateful for all that you did in helping us to locate our family, but..."

"Why have I taken such an interest in you? Probably because I saw in you something very similar to what Senor Dominguez saw. I saw it in the saloon that first day. There's a no-nonsense quality about you. You see something you want, and you go after it. Oh, it was only by accident that I happened to be talking to Manuel Dominguez one day. During our discussion he mentioned a young man named Bill Mulholland with whom he was quite impressed – a young man who was going to become an engineer. This, of course, piqued my interest in you even more. It seemed to verify my own opinion of you.

"Then, several months later, I happened to be attending a luncheon with several businessmen, many of whom are associated with the water company. During the course of the conversation the subject of *zanjero* operations arose. This led to a rather heated debate as to who had the greatest number of ditch handlers assigned to their area. Eventually the actual names of deputy *zanjeros* were read off so comparisons could be made as to the quality of each *zanjero's* performance. This part of the luncheon was becoming so boring I was about to excuse myself and depart when the name Mulholland was read from the roster. I stopped in my tracks and inquired as to the first name of this Mulholland person and was told that it was William. Further inquiry revealed your assigned work area. This, of course, immediately aroused suspicion. Your employers wanted to know why the county sheriff was interested in the identity of one of their employees. Realizing the spot I was placing you in I quickly assured them that you were not wanted for any crimes. In fact, you were a friend of mine, and I had lost track of you. When I departed, I was quite certain that everyone present was convinced that you are innocent of any wrongdoing."

Mulholland frowned and shook his head. "I hope so, Sheriff. I hope you haven't caused me to lose my job."

"Relax, William. This luncheon was over a month ago. If they haven't made any inquiries yet I'm sure they aren't going to."

They talked for several more minutes. Bill related to the sheriff the progress he had made to date in his engineering studies, as well as his desire to move ahead in the water company's hierarchy, though he was aware that such progress was a long way down the road.

"Who knows, William? Maybe it won't be so far as you think. Like you, I believe that Los Angeles is on the verge of a serious water crisis. It is inevitable that the water company is going to have to seek water from some other source than what flows into the Los Angeles River. And that will require fresh ideas from young engineers such as yourself.

"Look at it this way: you are already an employee of the water company, and I have also learned that your boss, Fred Eaton, has an eye on you and he likes what he sees. Just finish your studies and you will have a foot in the door."

Mulholland grinned shyly. "I've been so busy working and studying I guess I never had time to give to such thoughts. But the way you put it; it makes sense."

Sensing that Bill's attitude had become much more amiable he decided this was a good time to depart. Slapping a hand on his knee the sheriff arose from his chair. "Well, William, I've been here much longer than I intended. Guess I better be getting on my way."

Bill appeared disappointed. "What? This is Sunday, Sheriff. You have all afternoon to visit."

Mitchell offered a friendly smile. "Sunday may be a day off for you, William, as it is for most people. But not for a sheriff. Truth is, I don't get a day off. Right now, I have to go by the jail and check up on the prisoners – make sure the count is right and their supper has been properly ordered." This was not entirely true, but the lawman needed an excuse to depart.

"Yes sir," Bill said. "I understand."

Bill followed his guest out of the house and watched him mount his horse. Just as the sheriff was about to urge the roan to move, he reined up. "I'm curious, William. Did you happen to have an opportunity to vote for me in the last election?"

Bill looked up at the sheriff sheepishly. "No sir." He quickly followed this reply by saying, "I had every intention of voting for you. But when I went to the polls on election day, I was informed that I was not eligible to vote because I wasn't an American citizen." After a pause he added, "But I did try, sir."

Mitchell could not help but display a broad smile. "That's ok, William. You did just fine. At least you tried, and no one could ask for anything more." At that he lightly touched the horse in the ribs with his boot heels as he reined to turn the mount in the reverse direction, then slowly rode away from Bill's tiny residence.

Bill watched as his guest rode away. When he was out of sight Bill returned to where he had planted the seedling and began digging it up. Moving several more feet from the sycamore, he pushed the shovel into the ground and began digging a new home for the oak.

5

THE YEAR 1878 ended and the following year came and went. Bill kept himself immersed in his work and his studies. Each day brought him closer to realizing his dream of becoming an engineer.

In the closing days of 1879 Bill and his fellow deputy *zanjeros* worked along the *zanja* that led to the reservoir at Elysian Park. As they removed weeds and debris from the ditches in an effort to keep them clean and free flowing, it was not unusual to attract occasional idle spectators who seemed to enjoy watching the *zaneros* at work. They were generally nothing more than town loafers with nothing better to do, not unlike those who would hang around the barber shop and idly watch the barber cut hair, or hang around the pool hall to watch customers shoot pool. They were not present at the *zanjas* every day. Only on occasion one might show up. It was Bill's practice to ignore them; that is, unless they attempted to talk to him. At that point he would intentionally react with a rude response to shut them up. He had no time for idle talk. He kept his mind focused on his job.

One day Bill was busily engaged in removing some debris from the ditch when he heard a voice say, "What are you doing?"

Without looking up Bill replied in a surly tone, "None of your damn business!"

Bill then realized that the inquirer was on horseback, for he heard the sound of hoof beats moving away from him. He just shrugged and continued with his work.

A moment later a fellow worker approached and said, "Hey Bill, you know who that was who tried to talk to you?"

"No, and I don't care."

"Well, you should. That was William Hayes Perry himself, president of the water company!"

Suddenly Bill felt sick. Without another word he climbed out of the ditch. At first, he thought of returning to his house and packing his things and leaving. But he knew that was not the right thing to do. Taking a deep breath, he moved in the direction of the area office to turn in his time. There was no doubt in his mind that he was about to be fired.

At the office they were expecting him, for the company president had gotten there before Bill. When Bill offered his time sheet the man behind the counter smiled.

"So, you're William Mulholland?"

"Yes sir," Bill said meekly.

"Mister Hayes just left here moments ago," the man behind the counter said.

By this time Bill was numb to any further bad news, so he made no comment.

"He left this note," the man behind the counter continued, "which says, in effect, that you are to be promoted to foreman."

As Sheriff of Los Angeles County, Henry Mitchell carried a lot of weight in the area. He had a friendly nature and was politically astute. Most folks liked him. He was on a first name basis with practically all the big wigs in the water company. Knowing Henry like I did I would, frankly, be surprised if he didn't drop Bill Mulholland's name around at opportune moments – in subtle ways, of course. And he would also make it a point to mention Bill's intense engineering studies. Now, there are no records that I am aware of to back up what I just said. I'm simply going by what I knew about Henry and what he would be willing to do for his friend.

(Just as an afterthought: both Bill and Henry would deny with their dying breaths what I just related.)

BY EARLY 1880 Bill Mulholland was working at his new position as foreman of a crew that was installing twenty-two-inch pipe, running parallel to the west bank of the river and extending to the foot of the Buena Vista Reservoir. The reservoir itself was in the process of being enlarged.

In addition to the promotion, the company moved Bill farther west to a small house that was closer to his work. To say the new residence was a step up in accommodation, however, would be an exaggeration. It was a crude structure located west of Broadway. Though somewhat larger than his previous dwelling, his new residence had a less cozy feel to it. It didn't even have a stove. Fortunately, Bill's Uncle Richard Deakers provided him with one that tended to smoke up the house when in use. But once Bill put up new shelves and moved all his books, tables, desk and chairs into the new place he began to feel more at home. His tastes were simple, and as a bachelor, he had no one to please but himself. He was content.

As a foreman, Bill was able to occasionally mingle with surveyors and company engineers. And he was never shy about taking advantage of these encounters. He would pump them for information regarding water issues related to their professions. These engineers were at first taken aback by this young man's knowledge of some of the more intricate details pertaining to engineering in general and hydrology specifically. But none of them took offense. Quite the contrary; they found it refreshing that this young man held such a fascination regarding this field of work. And it wasn't long before Mulholland's name was known throughout the water company.

Bill Mulholland was also blessed with an excellent memory. Everything he learned in books and everything that he observed pertaining to the water system was locked in his memory in minute detail. This asset, as well as his strong work ethic, were soon rewarded by another promotion, then another.

In 1886, the superintendent that oversaw the large area of the company where Bill worked, dropped dead suddenly of a heart attack. After giving a great deal of thought as to whom the late superintendent's replacement might be, company President Perry, through the recommendation of others, named Bill Mulholland as the new superintendent. Eight years earlier Bill had been hired as a ditch digger, and now he had risen to the position of superintendent in the water company. His future was looking bright.

Bill was now on his way to making a name for himself. As superintendent he had well over a hundred men working for him, as well as several supervisors who saw to the day-to-day assignments for each worker. If Bill were so inclined, he could have spent his work days inside his cozy office, and let his supervisors see to the work in the field. But that wasn't his style. His was a hands-on nature. He had to be in the field – not as a direct supervisor but to assure himself that the overall operation was being carried out to his liking.

WHEN MULHOLLAND FIRST went to work as a ditch digger for the water company, his salary was a pittance compared to that of the average worker, but within ten years he was making a salary commensurate with that of any executive in a major business. But Bill's day-today habits had changed little. He was quite frugal and continued to live in the modest shack he had moved into upon being promoted to foreman. He managed to save a large portion of his salary, and by 1890 was able to live quite comfortably. It was that same year that another chapter in his life was about to spring upon him.

6

WHEN MULHOLLAND FIRST arrived in Los Angeles in 1877 the population of the city was 9,000. By 1890 it had swollen to 50,000, with no sign of a let-up in its growth, yet the Los Angeles River was still the city's main source of water. The citrus industry in and around the city was flourishing, which added to the strain on the water supply. Wells had been dug in various parts of the city, and reservoirs had been erected to store water during heavy rainfalls to be used during the dry spells. But the need for more water was incessant.

In the summer of 1890 Mulholland accompanied his workers to Crystal Springs, just north of Los Feliz and a short distance west of the Los Angeles River. The area immediately west of the springs was an extremely large land area owned by Colonel Griffith W. Griffith. Six years later he would donate four thousand acres of the land to the city of Los Angeles to be used as a park.

The job at Crystal Springs was a major endeavor and required the efforts of every one of Bill's one hundred men and their foremen. A camp was set up near a new housing tract development. Rather than travel back and forth between the office and the work site, Bill moved into the work camp. The task at hand was the laying of percolation pipes extending from Crystal Springs to land in the vicinity of Los Feliz.

Prior to laying the pipe, permission had to be obtained from the owners of the land. As the work moved southward Mulholland realized that it would be necessary to obtain permission from the owner of a tract of land that looked down upon the river before proceeding. The property was owned by a man named James Ferguson.

Attired in work clothes not unlike that of his subordinates, Bill walked up to the Ferguson residence and knocked on the front door. A long moment passed before the door opened, and standing before him was a young lady that he found most attractive.

"I…uh…I'm looking for the Ferguson residence," he announced, somewhat irritated by his lack of poise.

"This is the Ferguson residence," she replied, as she hid the amused smile at the man's discomfort.

"My name is Bill Mulholland, and I represent the Los Angeles Water Company. Is Mr. Ferguson in?"

"Yes, he is. Won't you come in?" Lillian Ferguson would later confess to her friends that she knew from the moment she first laid eyes on Bill Mulholland that he was the man she would marry.

It was a whirlwind courtship; then, on July 3, 1890, Bill and Lillie were wed. The ceremony took place in the Ferguson residence. Among the guests were Bill's Aunt Catherine and Uncle Richard Deakers. Henry Mitchell sent his regrets at being unable to attend. Legal matters had required him to be out of town on the day of the wedding. He did, however, send a beautiful arrangement of flowers.

The work at Crystal Springs continued until the job was finished, and only then did Bill and Lillie move into a home of their own located on a street that would one day be called North Broadway. Over the next three years they would have three children: one daughter and two sons.

FOR THE MOST PART, the year 1890 was a happy time for William Mulholland. But an incident occurred in the last month that would cause the year to end on a sad note.

He was sitting behind the desk in his office one Monday morning in early December when an assistant barged into the room without so much as a knock. Bill looked up to see an old friend from his *zanjero* days standing before him. In his hand was a folded newspaper.

"Have you heard the news, Boss?" the man asked, an expression of both shock and sadness on his face.

"No. What is it ... a busted pipe somewhere?"

The man responded by offering the newspaper he had been holding to the superintendent. Reaching across the desk, Mulholland took the paper and opened it. On the front page the headline read: *Former Sheriff Henry Mitchell Killed in Hunting Accident.*

Mulholland stared at the headlines for a long moment but made no comment. The messenger, sensing his boss' need to be alone, stepped out of the office, quietly closing the door behind him.

Bill turned his swivel chair to the right and stared, through misty eyes, out the office window. His thoughts raced back to the day he and Hugh first rode into town. Henry Mitchell was the first person to welcome them to Los Angeles. As undersheriff, Mitchell had been of valuable assistance in helping them locate their family members.

Though Bill saw little of Mitchell, he followed the sheriff's career as he was elected county sheriff. He had later learned that Mitchell had been keeping an eye on the young man who had become a ditch digger for the water company. A tear fell down Bill's cheek as he contemplated the probability of Henry's influence in the series of promotions Bill enjoyed in the water company.

This was only speculation on the superintendent's part, for, the fact was, he and Henry Mitchell had not seen one another since Mitchell's term as sheriff expired. He was aware that his friend, following his position as sheriff, served as undersheriff under his successor, and only recently returned to his law practice. And now he was dead – his life cut short by a bullet. He was forty-three years old.

AFTER BILL WAS promoted to superintendent, I didn't see much of him for several months. He was quite busy – either in his office or, more likely, overseeing one job or another on the far side of the city. Of course, I did read a great deal about him in the newspapers, and on at least a few occasions we ran across each other in the city library. Bill was a great reader, and he would visit the library to see if there were any new editions related to engineering. He liked to stay abreast of the latest innovations. Occasionally he would borrow some classic novels, such as Les Misérables. *But mostly, his interests centered around the various fields of engineering.*

As for Henry Mitchell, I hardly saw him at all after he finished his term as sheriff. I'm not sure how close he and Bill remained after Bill's promotion to superintendent. It might have been that the former sheriff felt that he had done as much as he could for the young engineer. I also doubt very much if either of them would have let their friendship ebb away. Needless to say, Bill was devastated by the premature passing of his friend.

After marrying Lillie Ferguson in 1890, Bill spent most of his free time with his family. In 1891 a daughter was born. They named her Rose Ellen. In 1892 Lillie gave birth to a son, whom they named William Perry. Two years later a second son, Thomas Ferguson, was born. Bill proved to be a most attentive husband and father.

Of course, the need for more water was a constant problem for the people of Los Angeles, for the city was growing in leaps and bounds. The search for additional water sources was an endless concern for William Mulholland.

Fred Eaton, the man who originally hired Bill as a ditch digger back in 1878, was elected to a two-year term as mayor of Los Angeles and served from 1898 to 1900. He ran on a platform of developing a new municipal water system, and a year later the city purchased the privately owned Los Angeles City Water Company. The city was now in the water business. At the urging of Mayor Eaton, William Mulholland was named superintendent and chief engineer of the municipally owned water company.

AT FIRST GLANCE, one might consider the friendship of Fred Eaton and William Mulholland most unusual. Born just three years after the end of the infamous potato famine in Ireland, when a million died from hunger, and another million fled the country to other parts of the world, Bill grew up in dire poverty. To escape the privation that was a part of life in his beloved Ireland, Bill went to sea, eventually settling in America. Poverty had stayed with him until going to work at the water company in Los Angeles.

Fred Eaton, by contrast, grew up in Los Angeles, a child of affluence. His father, Benjamin Smith Eaton, a Harvard graduate and lawyer, served for a time as Los Angeles district attorney, and later as a judge. He was also one of the founders of the city of Pasadena.

In addition to affluence, Fred was gifted with a high level of intelligence, and became a self-taught engineer. He went to work for the water company, and at the age of nineteen, became a superintendent in the company. It was in this position that, in 1878, he hired Bill Mulholland as a ditch digger.

As time passed Eaton watched this ambitious young man grow, both in his day-to-day work as well as his determined pursuit of an education in hydraulic engineering. Despite their diverse backgrounds, there was a kinship in the two men. Though there is no evidence that the two men ever became bosom buddies, as Bill rose in the ranks of the water company, they did become professional allies, possibly borne of mutual admiration, as well as concern for the future of Los Angeles.

BY 1900, THIRTEEN years after Mulholland first arrived in Los Angeles, the population had multiplied to eleven times what it was in 1877. It had risen to over 102,000 and was continuing to grow. The citrus industry was also expanding, which created an even greater need for water. The meager flow of water from the Los Angeles River simply could not meet the needs of Los Angeles, nor could the springs and reservoirs scattered in various parts of the city supply enough to quench the city's thirst. Fred Eaton and William Mulholland agreed that they must go outside the city in search of a source of the precious commodity.

MONDAY
March 12, 1928

11:40 A.M.

THE CURTISS JENNY landed on a hard-packed surface of dirt and sand a hundred yards east of Highway 14 in Mojave. Between the landing strip and the road was a run-down motor court that had seen better days.

When the plane came to a stop, Jeff alighted and proceeded to place chocks in front of and behind the wheels. With a rope, a long metal rod and a hammer he anchored the tail section to the ground as a precaution against gusts of wind that frequented the area.

The passenger slowly made his way out of the front seat and eased his way down to the ground. Approaching fifty-three years of age, he was slightly under six feet tall and had a slim build. His once dark hair was now mostly gray.

The pilot was securing the tail section to the ground as the older man walked past. Without stopping he said, "When you get through here, Jeff, meet me in the cafe."

"Yes sir," Jeff replied without looking up from his work. After securing the aircraft and stowing the hammer in a side compartment, the young man moved with a slight limp toward the motor court.

An inch taller than his uncle, and with a more muscular build, Jeff Kienast was two weeks shy of his 24th birthday. He had walked with a limp since childhood. When he was twelve years old Jeff was riding a horse on the family ranch when the horse stepped in a hole, throwing Jeff to the ground. Coming up behind him was a horse-drawn wagon being driven by a ranch hand. Before the driver could react the left front wheel rolled over Jeff's right foot, breaking bones that never healed properly, and Jeff had walked with a limp ever since. Fortunately, the injury had affected only his foot and not his knee. This allowed him to control the foot pedals of the aircraft. Without his beloved Jenny, Jeff would be lost. The fact that it was his right foot that suffered the injury was also fortunate, for it allowed him to mount a horse with little trouble from the left side. This was critical, for he lived on a working ranch owned by his father. It was the family's livelihood, and second only to flying, ranching was Jeff's reason for getting up in the morning.

The large ranch was a few miles outside of Bishop – a hundred and seventy miles north of where he stood at present. Jeff suddenly felt a longing to be home at this moment, and not being a party to whatever scheme that he feared was coming.

Limping past the motor court cottages, he turned right and moved past the front office and came to the modest café next door. The café and motel were owned by the same person, and the lack of cleanliness of one was matched by neglect of the other. Stepping inside, Jeff was not surprised by the two men who shared the table with his Uncle Emmett, for they had accompanied him on his drive from Owens Valley to Mojave. This brought a humorless smile to Jeff's face as he was reminded of his uncle's reluctance to fly any farther than necessary to accomplish whatever business he was on at the time. While the older man recognized the need to accompany his nephew on an aerial view of the dam, he had not been willing to accompany Jeff on the flight down from Bishop.

Emmett Hollister and his companions were the only customers in the room. Taking a deep breath and blowing it out in a sigh, Jeff moved toward them.

Albert Slocomb, tall and lean, with cruel eyes and a perpetual frown on his face, sat next to Merle Clinton, sandy haired, with a quick, but insincere, smile directed at no one in particular, were Hollister's companions. Jeff had seen the two of them in Independence a few times but paid them little mind. They had struck him as town loafers.

"Ah, Jeff!" His uncle greeted. "Pull up a chair and join us."

"No, thank you, sir. I just dropped by to tell you that I'll be leaving now." When his uncle made no reply, Jeff continued, "Since I did what you asked me to do, there's no need for me to stick around."

"Don't you want to grab a bite to eat before you go?"

"No, thank you." Staring directly into his uncle's eyes, Jeff added, "After our morning's work, I don't have much of an appetite."

This brought an ugly grimace to Emmett's face, and he glared angrily at his nephew. "Then go ... and be damned!"

As Jeff turned to go, his uncle called after him. "But if you breathe a word of this to anyone, you'll sorely regret it! What we're doing is for the good of the people of Owens Valley." He paused, then added, "Besides, you're in this just as much as we are!"

"Not hardly! You asked me to take you on a sightseeing tour of the reservoir and dam. Nothing more." Jeff's anger caused him to momentarily forget that Emmett Hollister was his blood kin. "Maybe I'm slow, but it wasn't until we were in the air and heading toward the dam that I began to feel uncomfortable about the whole trip. I then realized what you were up to." Another thought then occurred to him. "And what about the lives of those families who live in Francisquito Canyon? If anything happens to the dam, those folks won't have a chance! They have as much right to live as the folks in Owens Valley!"

Hollister stared hard at his nephew. "I guess that's the price to be paid for living near that Babylon they call Los Angeles."

Jeff had heard his uncle refer to Los Angeles as "Babylon," but the reference meant little to him. He stared speechless at his uncle for several seconds before turning to go. Stepping out of the café, he stopped at the office of the motor court to purchase enough gasoline for his return trip to Bishop. Twenty minutes later he was flying north toward home.

II:
OWENS VALLEY
1904

7

AN HOUR BEFORE sunset Bill Mulholland pulled the reins on the team of mules, bringing the buckboard to a stop. It had been a twenty-mile ride from the mercantile in Cantil, where they purchased food and filled their water keg, to the entrance to Jawbone Canyon. It would be another ten miles proceeding north through the canyon before Mulholland brought the team to a halt.

"Why did you stop?" The question came from Fred Eaton, who sat on the seat beside Mulholland. "We can go another few miles before dark."

Bill studied his companion, then slowly tied the reins around the brake handle. Breathing a deep sigh, he said, "These mules have had a long, hard day. They need a rest." Pausing briefly, he added, "And so do I."

The trek through the desert had been Fred Eaton's idea. On a camping trip in the Sierras a few years earlier he had seen a lake in Owens Valley, where fresh, clean water filled it each spring with melted snow from the peaks of the High Sierras. While some of the water was used to irrigate the crops of the farms in the valley, most of the lake's contents would evaporate during the hot months of the summer. It seemed a shame that so much was being wasted, while the growing community of Los Angeles was desperate for good, clean water. There had to be a way of purchasing some of the precious commodity from the residents of the valley and transporting it to Los Angeles, while leaving an ample supply for the locals.

An hour later, their camp set up and a fire going, the two men sat cross-legged on the ground eating their supper from tin plates. They had each found a flat rock on which to set their tin coffee cups.

Both men were silent as Bill took in his surroundings. Gazing off to the southwest, he studied the landscape and tried to picture the tremendous task that lay before them. This would be the general route of the aqueduct – down the length of Jawbone Canyon, then through the Tehachapi Mountains before the final trek to Los Angeles.

It was dusk, and the last rays of the sun had dipped behind the Tehachapi Mountain range off to the southwest, creating a colorless silhouette of the peaks that rose as high as seven thousand feet.

"If things go well with the people of Owens Valley, we should immediately put together a team to come here and survey the land in preparation for constructing the aqueduct."

"Well, that chore will have to be handled by you," Fred replied. "As you know, I will be leaving for Washington, D.C. to obtain permission to build the aqueduct. We can plan what needs to be done, but, of course, we can't actually begin construction until we have official permission.

His jaw set firmly, Bill stared at his friend for several seconds before saying, "I don't care how many arms you have to twist in Washington, this project has got to go through. There are 103,000 souls in Los Angeles who are depending on this water. I know of no other alternative to getting water down to the city."

Fred made no reply. He knew the stress his friend was experiencing. He felt it himself. Within a few years the population in and around the city would exceed half a million people. They were depending on this water. He smiled inwardly as he realized that the population issue would be his strongest argument with the powers that be in Washington.

Finishing his meal, Mulholland set his plate aside and stretched his arms upward and twisted his torso. "Gotta get the kinks out. Guess I'm getting too old for this sort of thing."

Eaton regarded his companion, then asked, "How old are you, Bill?"

"This month, September eleventh, I'll turn forty-nine."

"I don't believe it!" Eaton exclaimed. "We're practically the same age." When his companion offered no reply, he added, "You're just a year older than me!" He shook his head and grinned. "Why do I look so much younger than you?"

Mulholland stared at his friend for a long moment before returning the grin. "I suppose it's because of the lives we have each led. While you were still licking your silver spoon, I was swabbing the decks of three masted schooners. And while you were sitting quite comfortably in your office at the water company, I was outside, digging ditches." Following a pause, he added, "That sort of life takes its toll on a man."

Fred Eaton regarded his companion for a long moment before replying, "I suppose it does, Bill." After another pause, he added soberly, "You have sure come a long way, and I admire you for it."

Mulholland offered a slow smile. "I have the same feelings about you, Fred."

SHORTLY AFTER DAWN the following morning the two men resumed their ride northward through Jawbone Canyon, the mules trudging slowly in the loose sand of the Mojave Desert. With Fred Eaton at the reins, they stopped for the night in Inyokern. Two more long days and they would be at Owens Lake.

The trip by buckboard had been Fred's idea. He wanted his engineer friend to see firsthand the general route of the aqueduct that would carry the water down to Los Angeles. Conceiving the aqueduct was Eaton's idea. Designing and constructing it would fall on the shoulders of Mulholland, who took extensive notes regarding terrain, rock formations and soil content along the route.

Through tough negotiations with the city officials, most of whom Eaton knew on a personal basis, he convinced them that Los Angeles was facing a catastrophic water crisis if something was not done soon to bring the precious commodity to the city. He then introduced his proposal to bring water south from Owens Lake. Studies had shown that there was more than enough water to meet the needs of the city, as well as the needs of the communities surrounding the lake. It was a tough sell, for the cost of the project was prohibitive, but necessary. Eventually the city counsel approved funding for the project. Of course, much of the proposal depended upon the federal government's willingness to allocate federal lands, through which the aqueduct would traverse, before the project could even get off the ground.

IT WAS AFTER dark two days later when Mulholland brought the buckboard to a stop in front of a livery stable in Lone Pine. After paying the proprietor to feed, water and shelter the mules for the night, as well as safely storing the wagon and its contents, the two travelers went in search of a place to eat, followed by baths and rooms with comfortable beds.

During the weeks prior to their departure from Los Angeles, Fred Eaton had been in communication with the city and county officials regarding the purchase of water from the lake and was assured that a community meeting would be arranged to discuss the matter.

8

THE FOLLOWING MORNING, having finished breakfast, Mulholland and Eaton stepped out of the diner and stood for a moment looking across the street in the direction of the hotel where they had spent the night. But their westward gaze extended far beyond the hotel and rested upon the High Sierra mountain range.

"Can you make out that peak just to the right of two smaller ones?"

Fred Eaton asked his companion.

"There are a lot of peaks up there," his friend replied.

"Well, just focus on the one that seems to be higher than the others."

Bill Mulholland studied the mountain range for a long moment, then replied, "Yeah, I see the one you're talking about." He glanced briefly at his companion. "What about it?"

"That, my friend, is the summit of Mount Whitney. Just shy of fifteen thousand feet, Mount Whitney is the highest mountain peak in the United States."

"Even higher than any of the ones in the Rockies?"

"There isn't a mountain peak in any of the forty-five states that is higher than what you're looking at right now." Following a pause, he added, "Come this winter the whole mountain range will be covered by several feet of snow. In the spring that snow will melt, and a large portion of the water will flow down into the Owens River and fill the lake. The people in the valley cannot possibly use all the water. There is no reason why they shouldn't share some of it."

"When are we supposed to have our meeting with the powers that be?" Bill asked.

"Tomorrow."

"Where will it be held?"

"In Independence, the county seat."

"And where is Independence?"

"It's about fifteen or sixteen miles north of here." Fred breathed a sigh, then said, "There is no public transportation that I'm aware of, so we'll probably have to climb back in the buckboard early tomorrow morning and allow a few hours to make the trip."

"Why don't we leave now and get there this afternoon?" Bill suggested. "That way we can get a hotel room, take a bath and shave, and be ready first thing in the morning. Did they indicate what time the meeting will be?"

"Ten a.m."

Bill shrugged. "All the more reason we need to get there today,"

TWO HOURS LATER, their luggage all loaded in the bed of the buckboard and a sack of dry food and a canteen of water sitting on the seat between them, Fred Eaton and Bill Mulholland were on the road, heading north toward Independence. Taking their time, they arrived at a hotel in Independence at three p.m. While Fred took their luggage into the lodging, Bill drove the team to a livery, unhitched the mules, paid the stable man then walked to the hotel.

After shaving, taking baths and putting on fresh, clean clothes, they proceeded to the hotel desk, where they learned that the county courthouse, where the meeting was to take place, was only two blocks from the hotel. They arrived to find that the building was practically empty. A clerk at the lobby counter informed them that the meeting would take place in the Board of Supervisors' hearing room and was still set for ten a.m. the following day.

UPON ENTERING THE hearing room several minutes before ten o'clock the following morning Mulholland and Eaton were taken aback somewhat by the numerous attendees who had shown up for the meeting. Bill estimated that at least fifty people had been crowded into the large room, the vast majority of whom were middle-aged to older men, though there were a few women and younger attendees scattered among them.

Sitting in the back row was 25-year-old Frank Kienast. Sitting to his left was his wife, Anna. To the left of Anna was her older brother, Emmett Hollister.

Sitting at the front of the room in chairs facing the audience were members of the Inyo County Board of Supervisors. Several others were seated near the supervisors. One of the members of the board rose from his chair and held his hands up, signaling for silence.

"Good morning ladies and gentlemen. I am glad to see so many of our citizens taking an interest in the proposal by the city of Los Angeles to purchase some of the water from the Owens River.

"As I look around the room, I see representatives from Olancha, Lone Pine, Independence … " he paused briefly then added, "Oh, yes. I see Frank Kienast and his lovely wife, Anna." He smiled broadly and asked, "Tell me, Frank, are you here representing the town of Bishop?"

Frank Kienast slowly stood and returned the smile. "No, Herb. Not in an official capacity. We're just here to see what the to-do is all about." He then sat back down.

"Well, Frank, we're glad to have you."

As Frank was sitting down, he turned briefly toward Emmett, and noticed an angry scowl on his face."

"What's wrong, Emmett?" He whispered.

Emmett turned toward Frank. "Nothing. Nothing at all."

"Before we introduce our guests from Los Angeles," Herb resumed, "I would like to remind you of the Reclamation Act of 1902, passed by the U.S. Senate and signed into law by President Roosevelt. It says, in effect, that arid lands in the western part of the country where irrigation is needed for farming, et cetera, will be partially funded by the federal government.

"So, keep this in the back of your minds when listening to the request by our two guests." Following a brief pause, Herb continued, "And with that, may I present the former mayor of Los Angeles Fred Eaton, and William Mulholland, head of the Los Angeles Water Company."

When Bill and Fred rose from their seats they were met by sporadic applause, with fewer than half of the attendees clapping a welcome for the visitors from Los Angeles.

Showing no surprise at the tepid welcome by the attendees, Herb invited the two guests to the front of the room and gave them the floor.

"Good morning," Fred began. "I have no doubt that many of you are unaware of why my good friend, Bill Mulholland, and I have come here, hat-in-hand, to appeal to you for help.

"As most of you know, Los Angeles is suffering from a severe water shortage. At one time, not too many years ago, the Los Angeles River, though never known for carrying more than a few feet of water in any given year, did, in fact, provide sufficient amounts to support a population of a few thousand souls in and around the city. But, over the past few decades Los Angeles has grown significantly. Today that population is well over one hundred thousand. In spite of the fact that the city has turned to every resource available, such as digging wells and searching for springs, to bring more water, it is falling far short of what is needed. In the next decade that population will exceed a half million."

Just as he was about to continue, a hand arose in the last row. Fred gestured to the man as he stood up. The speaker was Emmett Hollister.

"Just what is it," Hollister began in a hostile tone, "that makes Los Angeles so special that people seem to flock to it?" He grinned, but it was not friendly. "I've been there and, frankly, I wasn't impressed." This brought a few chuckles from the audience.

"Well, for one thing, the climate, to most residents, is ideal. The winters are very mild, and the summers, for the most part are not too hot. There is also a railroad that runs between San Francisco and Los Angeles, connecting the city with the rest of the country. The citrus industry, primarily oranges, is promising." Following a short pause, he added, "And will be more promising with more water.

"And last but not least, Los Angeles is one of very few cities that can boast of two sea ports – one in San Pedro and another in Santa Monica." Breathing a sigh, Fred added, "The only thing Los Angeles is lacking is sufficient water to support the growing population."

"Well now, that sounds like you have a huge problem," Hollister smirked as he sat down.

"Yes, it is a huge problem," Fred replied. "And that is why we are here. You folks are blessed with an abundance of water." Following a pause, he added, "And we would like to buy some of it from you." He stopped to emphasize his next statement before continuing. "If any of you own property around the lake, especially land south of it, we are interested in purchasing it from you. And if you are not interested in selling, perhaps you would be interested in a long-term lease on your property.

"Oh, I might add, for those of you from down south in Olancha area, this also applies to you."

"What about the Reclamation Act that Herb was mentioning?" someone in the audience asked.

"Well, the way I understand the act, it seems to primarily address the lands off to the east of here – nearer the Inyo Mountains. It is mostly focused on the inhabitants – especially the Indian tribes – with most of the money going toward land owners digging their own wells."

For the better part of a minute Fred waited for the whispering, mumbling and general discontent in the audience to run its course. At length a member of the audience stood and was recognized by Herb.

"That's not what we were led to believe," he protested.

Fred shrugged. "Well, that is the way I read it. Of course, I could very well be wrong. But I cannot imagine the government just passing out money to anyone living in the area, especially where a great quantity of water is already available to you just for the taking."

Following another moment of mumbling in the audience, Fred resumed. "Folks, Los Angeles is in a bind. We need a decision now. If you turn us down we will have no choice but to go to Arizona and seek permission to take water from the Colorado River. This requires a great deal more negotiating and tons of paper work, so we would prefer to work something out with you. You are fellow Californians." Offering a grin, he added, "And I must say, Owens Valley is a lot closer than the Colorado River."

"As soon as we return to Los Angeles, I will be going to Washington, D.C. to get the ball rolling. So, I need a commitment from you before we return to Los Angeles. If your answer is no, then I will be going to Arizona. That is how critical the situation is."

"How long will you be in town?" Herb wanted to know.

"We can stay a few days, but then we have to leave. If you decide to work with us, I will have several papers for those of you to sign who will be directly affected, or if you have land to sell. Perhaps Herb can arrange an office from which we can work."

Turning to Mulholland, he asked, "Bill, do you have anything you would like to add?"

"Just this," Bill said as he slowly got to his feet, "If we get permission to use your water, upon our return to Los Angeles, I will begin immediately surveying the land south of here and mapping out a route for the aqueduct that will deliver the water down to Los Angeles."

"That must be two hundred miles!" a man in the audience exclaimed.

"More like two hundred forty miles," Bill corrected.

"How do you expect to get the water over the Tehachapi range?"

"We will go *through* the mountains."

"Well, I declare!" the man said before sitting down.

"No one said it would be easy," Bill quipped with a grin.

9

WHEN THE MEETING was over, Frank and Anna Kienast returned to Bishop in their carriage. Kienast owned a sizable horse ranch a few miles southwest of town that he had inherited from his father.

Before returning to their home, they had to make a stop in town to pick up their infant son, Jeffrey, who was being watched by their close friends, Jim and Martha Lundstrum. Jim was also Frank's accountant.

The Lundstrums' baby daughter, Angela, was the same age as Jeffrey. Anna and Martha would often joke that the youngsters would grow up and marry. The two families would then be relatives.

It was late afternoon when the young Kienast family arrived at their home. It was a beautiful single-story house, made of pine, painted white. The shutters and eaves were bright blue. In the front of the house a bed of roses graced each side of the driveway. Behind the house were all the out buildings needed to comprise a working ranch, and beyond the acreage were the magnificent peaks of the High Sierras.

After driving the carriage to the large barn in the back, Frank joined his wife and child inside the house.

Anna had begun preparing supper when the sound of a carriage came from the front of the house. Frank, who was sitting in the living room, rose and walked to the door. Just as he opened it he was surprised to see his brother-in-law, Emmett Hollister.

"Emmett, it seems ages since I last saw you! " He greeted with a good-natured grin. "Come on in. We were just about to have supper. I hope you'll join us."

"Thanks, Frank, I'd like that, if it isn't too much trouble."

In spite of the friendly exchange, the arrival of Anna's brother was both unexpected and quite unusual, for the family was not close, and the visit, Frank guessed, would involve some request from Emmett. Though he lived just outside of Independence, Anna rarely saw her brother. The modest, last-minute supper was eaten, for the most part, in silence. It had been only a few hours since the three of them had been sitting together at the meeting in Independence, so there was no news to be exchanged.

"So, tell me, Emmett," Frank began as he set his napkin on the table after finishing his meal, "What brings you up this way?"

Emmett made a face as he stared at his brother-in-law. "Do I need an excuse to drop by for a visit with my sister?"

Frank offered a patient smile. "Emmett, we were together all morning. That was the first we had seen of you in months." Returning Emmett's cold stare, he added, "So yes. This visit is quite unexpected."

Anna had been silent throughout the meal. Her brother was cold and insensitive. There was nothing she could say that would ease the tension that was brewing, so she remained silent.

"All right, I'll tell you why I came." The surliness remained in his voice. "I came to see Anna – to ask her what she would be willing to take for her share of the property Papa left us."

Anna stared questioningly at her brother. "Property? What property?"

"You know. The ten acres near Lone Pine – south of the lake."

Anna slowly shook her head in an attempt to make sense of the question. "I'm sorry, Emmett. I don't recall any property being left to us."

"Well, it isn't much, but there it is."

Anna and Frank exchanged glances, then she said, "Would you excuse us, Emmett? I need to speak privately with my husband. You can go wait in the living room."

After Emmett went into the living room, Anna led Frank into the bedroom down the hall.

"Do you have any idea what he's talking about?" Frank asked.

"Like I said in the kitchen, I know nothing about any land," Anna began. "As you know, Emmett is the spitting image of our father. I was quite young when our mother died, so it was just the three of us." Following a wry smile, she added, "It wasn't easy living with *two* Emmetts. I was just glad you came along and rescued me from them." She gazed affectionately at her husband. "I am so blessed to be part of your life. And to top it off, you gave me such a wonderful son."

"So, what do you think?" Frank asked. "How do you want to handle this inherited land situation?"

"Why don't we just give him my share, Frank? God has been so good to us, and it's not like we need it."

Frank shrugged. "If that is what you want to do, it's fine with me."

Upon returning to the living room where Anna announced their decision, a complete change seemed to come over her brother. The surliness vanished immediately and was replaced by a placating smile.

"Oh, Sis," he began. "You don't know what this means to me. Your generosity touches me deeply." Reaching into his pocket, he withdrew some papers. "This is the deed. If I could just get a signature releasing your share to me, it's all settled."

Within a minute after the deed was signed, Emmett was climbing into his carriage. He had some fast work to do before those men from Los Angeles departed.

THE NEXT FEW days were busy for Eaton and Mulholland. Word from the meeting had gotten out to virtually everyone affected by the agreement between the Los Angeles Water Company and Owens Valley residents. Though there were hold-outs, many of the affected citizens were quite willing to sell those rights. Among them was Emmett Hollister. In his case, Hollister was not content to sell the water rights, but to sell his ten acres – if the price was right. Eaton expressed interest but informed Hollister that he was not authorized to make any purchases until the city of Los Angeles approved the funds.

"When will that be?" Hollister asked.

"Hopefully, it will be right after Mr. Mulholland and I return to Los Angeles." Following a pause, Eaton added with a smile, "They are hurting for water down there, so I am quite sure the money will be forthcoming rather quickly."

Hollister was not happy with the response, but he grudgingly accepted Eaton's assurance. With the ever-present scowl on his face, he departed.

After obtaining the assurance that enough land owners were willing to sell all their water rights, Mulholland and Eaton, two days later, departed Independence. The first two hours of their ride south in the buckboard went quietly as each man was lost in his own thoughts. In Lone Pine they purchased enough food, water and other necessities for the long ride through Jawbone Canyon. Fred was anxious to get back to Los Angeles, but Bill insisted on taking the time to record necessary notes regarding the geologic issues so the aqueduct builders would be prepared for the challenging work ahead.

Three days later they arrived in Cantil, where the buckboard and mules were returned to the owner. They paid for the rental of the wagon and team, as well as for storage of Fred's 1903 Ford Model B auto in which the two men would return to Los Angeles. It would be a few years before a highway ran from Mojave through Lone Pine, Independence and Bishop. There was, however, a rugged pack trail that connected those towns, and it was on this bumpy route that the Ford would travel until it reached Mojave. From there it would be a long ride home, but, unlike the hard bench of the buckboard, the seats in the car were padded.

MONDAY
March 12, 1928

4:00 P.M.

THE CURTISS JENNY'S tail waved slightly as it approached the runway one hundred yards behind the Kienast ranch house. With full flaps, the biplane straightened as it glided to the ground. Jeff Kienast taxied the craft to the end of the runway, then turned the plane to the left and brought it to a stop in front of a large wooden structure that was the hangar.

After the better part of four hours flying there was stiffness in his legs and back as he alighted from the craft. Removing his flying cap, which, like the Jenny herself, was a relic of the late war, he turned toward the ranch house. As he did so, he saw his father, Frank, walking hurriedly toward him, a worried look on his face.

At forty-nine years of age, Frank Kienast looked ten years younger. His hair had yet to turn grey, and, physically, he kept himself trim and fit. Seeing Frank Kienast worried was a rare sight – not since his wife, Anna, had passed away from a brain tumor in 1924, had Jeff seen his father in such a state. Anna was forty-three years old when she died. Jeff was twenty at the time.

"Hi Dad," Jeff greeted as he limped toward his father. "What's wrong?"

"What's wrong?" Frank replied as they approached one another. "You've been gone since early yesterday! I've been worried sick about you!" Glancing toward the plane, he added, "I always worry when you go up in that contraption."

"Sorry, Dad," Jeff replied meekly. "I was doing a favor for Uncle Emmett."

"Emmett," Frank repeated, a note of disapproval in his voice. "So, the two of you have been flying around since yesterday?"

"No sir. I met him yesterday down in Mojave. He wanted me to fly him over that new dam where they're storing the water they took from the Owens River."

"Why didn't he fly down with you?"

Jeff tried to force a grin. "Uncle Emmett doesn't like flying any more than you do. He drove down with two other men. They stayed in a motor lodge in Mojave while Uncle Emmett and I took the plane over San Francisquito Canyon, where that new dam is."

"Why the Sam Hill did he want to do that?" Frank Kienast and Emmett Hollister had a mutual dislike, and they had rarely seen one another since Anna's death. The only times Frank saw his former brother-in-law was when Emmett wanted a favor.

Jeff stared at the ground – his face downcast. "Can we go inside the house, Dad? There's something I need to talk to you about."

"Sure," he replied, recognizing the desperate look on his son's face, his own irritation was forgotten.

TWENTY MINUTES LATER they sat across from one another, a cup of freshly brewed coffee in hand. "Well, son, you have the floor. So, tell me, what's up with you, Uncle Emmett and the dam?"

"You, me and most of Owens Valley know full well that Uncle Emmett was a party to sabotaging sections of the aqueduct a few years back, though no one could prove it."

"Yes. Ever since he lost that piece of land of his to the folks in Los Angeles for a fraction of what he had hoped to get he has had it in for them."

"Yes sir," Jeff replied. "And since we know that he is capable of doing damage to their property, I'm concerned that he has plans to damage that dam. The terrifying part is that there is a small village down stream from the dam. If water gets loose, those people's lives could be in danger." He breathed a forlorn sigh before continuing. "When I told him about the people down below he just shrugged it off as if it was no concern of his."

"Well," Frank replied, "Your uncle is capable of a lot of things, but murder is not one of them. None of the acts of sabotage he was involved in when they were building the aqueduct caused any bodily injury." Following a pause, he added, "Of course, there were people injured in a few of the bombings, but, so far as I know, your uncle had nothing to do with those."

Jeff shook his head but made no comment.

"I'll tell you what, son. It's too late today, but first thing tomorrow morning we'll take a ride down to the sheriff's office in Independence, and you can relate what you witnessed this morning."

Jeff nodded but made no reply. He said a silent prayer that tomorrow morning would not be too late.

III:
THE
AQUEDUCT
1905-1921

10

DURING THIS PERIOD Lillie Mulholland gave birth to a daughter whom they named Ruth. In early 1903 she gave birth to a son. They named him Richard James. He was not a healthy child, and in mid-1905, Richard passed away. He was two-and-a-half years old. It was a sad time for the whole Mulholland family. Richard's siblings grieved the loss as children will. Because they had little time to get to know their baby brother, the grief passed. The loss hit Lillie the hardest. She had given birth to the child and had nursed him and cared for him during his illness. She was a strong woman, however, and eventually the pain of the loss began to fade. As for Bill, he coped with the sad loss the only way he knew. He threw himself into his work.

THE VOTERS OF Los Angeles County approved $1.5 million dollars for the purchase of land and water rights needed to start the aqueduct. Within a short time, enough of these rights were obtained from Owens Valley residents to dissuade the Federal Bureau of Reclamation from going through with the irrigation project.

On September 10, 1905, William Mulholland celebrated his fiftieth birthday with Lillie and their children, aboard a British ship moored in Sausalito, California. He was in a celebratory mood, for the aqueduct bond had been approved, and work was about to begin. He was also in the bay area to obtain supplies for the mammoth undertaking.

On June 26, 1906, after hearing objections from representatives of Owens Valley and private water interests, President Theodore Roosevelt penned a letter which read, in part, *"... I am also impressed by the fact that the chief opposition to this bill, aside from the opposition of a few settlers in Owens Valley (whose interest is genuine, but whose interest must unfortunately be disregarded in view of the infinitely greater interest to be served by putting the water in Los Angeles) comes from certain power companies whose object evidently is for their own pecuniary interest to prevent the municipality from furnishing its own water."*

The cancellation of the irrigation project had a deleterious effect on the value of property in Owens Valley, and Fred Eaton jumped at the opportunity to purchase land at a fraction of what it might otherwise have been worth. Among those who were outraged was Emmett Hollister. When he approached Eaton on the matter, the former mayor of Los Angeles calmly replied that, if Hollister refused to sell his land, the water project would simply bypass it and proceed south on public land by a slightly diverted route. Hollister was livid, but he agreed to sell at the price offered, though it was considerably less than what he had hoped to get. It was the birth of a grudge that he would nurse for years.

In the coming months the plans for the aqueduct began to take shape. Joining the Mulholland-Eaton team was Joseph B. Lippincott, a highly respected engineer, topographer and hydrographer. For the next five years the three of them worked daily to give birth to an aqueduct project that would later be celebrated as one of the two greatest engineering achievements in modern history – second only to the Panama Canal.

IT WAS LATE EVENING when the two-year-old 1906 Packard Touring Sedan came to a stop in front of the Victorian house at Sixth and Cummings Streets in Boyle Heights. It was a large mansion-type structure in an upper-class area of East Los Angeles and was now the home of the Mulholland family. Bill often stood in the street and stared at the palatial structure and marveled at its size. His thoughts would go back to his first days in Los Angeles, when he worked as a ditch digger for the water company, and lived in a tiny shack that would have easily fit inside any of the bedrooms of his present residence. Bill was not a snob, but he marveled at all that had come his way in the past three decades.

He alighted from the vehicle and held the door open for Lillie. They were returning from a performance at the two-year-old Mason Opera House on South Broadway in downtown Los Angeles. Mulholland then leaned toward the driver.

"Pick me up at seven tomorrow morning," he instructed.

"Yes sir," the driver responded, then drove away in the company's executive car.

It had been an all-together pleasant day for the "Chief," as he was known by employees at the water company. He had spent the day with Lillie and their three children and had played games with each of them throughout the day. The family enjoyed a delicious dinner, which included each child's favorite dish. The trip to the opera was a special outing for Lillie and Bill.

The following morning, he would be leaving for an extended stay in Jawbone Canyon, south of Owens Lake, where work had already begun on the aqueduct. He was not sure when he would return home.

The year was 1908, and the city of Los Angeles had approved an additional twenty-three million dollars for construction of the aqueduct. As many as four thousand workers were now on the job. Work was broken up into different places, and progress was apparent throughout the region, from Lone Pine to the foothills of the Tehachapi mountains.

THE DRIVE TOOK them through the San Fernando Valley, then onto the Sierra Highway, which was a long dirt road that proceeded through Lancaster, Mojave and as far north as Lake Tahoe.

When, at last, they reached the entrance to Jawbone Canyon, twenty-two miles north of Mojave, the driver turned the Packard west, into the canyon. As they pulled up to the work camp, which served as the project headquarters, one of the foremen rushed up to the car just as it came to a stop.

"Hey, Boss, you gotta see this!" the foreman exclaimed excitedly as Mulholland stepped out of the Packard. Mulholland allowed himself to be led by the foreman to a mule-drawn wagon. At the foreman's suggestion, Mulholland climbed aboard.

"Where are we going?" he asked.

"You'll see," a brief pause followed. "It's better if I show you instead of trying to describe it."

"Did something go wrong?" the Boss wanted to know.

"No! Just the opposite!"

Several minutes later the foreman pulled on the reins and the mules came to a halt. Twenty feet ahead Mulholland stared unbelievingly at the sight before him. It was a huge, oddly shaped machine with a canopy on top. Beneath the canopy a man sat in a seat, appearing to be operating several levers.

"What is that thing?" he asked.

"It's a tractor."

"What does it do?" The Boss was beginning to lose his patience.

"It does just about everything! It can move large amounts of dirt and can even carry heavy machinery and such to wherever you want them."

"How? It doesn't have any wheels."

Standing up in the wagon, the foreman began waving his arms, attempting to get the attention of the man sitting atop the machine. A moment later the man was standing in front of the foreman and Mulholland.

"The Boss, here, would like a demonstration as to how this contraption operates."

"What would you like for it to do?" the man wanted to know.

The foreman looked around until he noticed a large wagon filled with various heavy machine parts. Pointing to the huge wagon, he said, "Hook it up to the tractor and pull it over to that hill." He pointed to a fairly steep mound fifty yards away. "Tow the wagon to the top then bring it back down."

Several minutes later the contraption was pulling the heavily laden trailer toward the hill. Glancing at the boss, the foreman read his thoughts. "You'll notice that, instead of wheels, it moves along on wide treads that do not get bogged down in sand or mud or practically anything else."

Without stopping at the base of the hill, the machine began climbing, effortlessly, up the steep grade. At the top, which was flat, like a mesa, and was spacious enough for the operator to turn both tractor and trailer around, then proceed down the steep grade. It moved slowly, but effortlessly, to the bottom of the hill, then stopped several feet in front of Mulholland. The operator stepped down from the machine and joined the two observers.

"Boss," the foreman began, "can you imagine how many mules it would take to pull a heavy load like the one this machine just carried up?" He paused briefly, then added, "An hour from now those poor mules would still be struggling to get to the top."

"What do you call that contraption?" Mulholland asked.

"It's called a caterpillar."

"Caterpillar?" The Boss asked. "You mean like the bug?"

"Yes sir," the operator replied.

"Why do they call it that?"

"Well, the way I heard, it happened like this: Benjamin Holt, who owns the factory that makes farm tractors, decided the machines would function better on tracks, instead of wheels. So, he designed and built one. After it was tested and performed to Holt's satisfaction, he arranged for the company's photographer to accompany him to where the tractor was working on a nearby farm.

"As they approached the area where the tractor had been working, the photographer studied it for a moment then declared that it must be broken. Then it started moving forward, yet the photographer could not see the large wheels turning. As you know, most rear tractor wheels are almost as tall as the tractor itself. Then Mr. Holt explained that there were no wheels. The tractor was driven by tracks that wrapped around gears at the lower part of the machine. There were crops growing between the onlookers and the tractor, blocking any view of the revolving tracks. The photographer exclaimed that the machine moved like a giant caterpillar crawling on the ground. Mr. Holt was amused by the reporter's observation, and the more he thought about it the more he liked it." The foreman paused for effect, then added, "And that's what they are now called." He shrugged before concluding, "I'm not so sure the name will stick, but, for now, these machines are called caterpillars."

"Besides hauling large loads up and down hills, what else are they good for?" the boss wanted to know.

"Sir, that was just a simple demonstration," the foreman replied. "They can carry almost anything anywhere! For instance, every piece of large, heavy equipment that is delivered by the railroad, we have to disassemble it and haul the parts by mule train from the railroad, then several miles across the canyon – up and down sandy hills, around boulders and across deep ruts made by flash floods, to where the construction site is. It's a long, difficult process – and it's time-consuming. Then, after the equipment arrives, we have to spend time reassembling it." The foreman nodded toward the caterpillar. "If we had a fleet of those, it wouldn't require disassembling anything. The equipment would arrive all ready to go to work." The foreman smiled inwardly for he knew he had the Boss's attention. "Even something as big as a steam shovel could be loaded onto a heavy wagon, then hooked up to this monster, and carried out here with little effort."

"What kind of fuel do they run on? It obviously isn't steam powered."

"Well, they do have steam-powered tractors, but this one runs on gasoline, just like our cars," the foreman replied. "I understand Mr. Holt is looking into diesel power. They are using it in Europe, but it isn't well known – or available – in the U.S. Someday it will be, but not yet. So, for now, the Holt factory is manufacturing them to be run on gasoline and steam."

Mulholland studied the ugly machine for a full minute, then announced, "I like it. Check into what the cost is for the gasoline powered machines. If the price is reasonable, order a few. We'll give them a try."

THE ENSUING MONTHS passed rapidly in Jawbone Canyon. Several miles of pipe was laid, seated inside miles of trenches that were from six to eight feet deep. During those months three Caterpillars arrived at the construction site and were immediately put into service. Evidence of their efficiency was immediate. They easily moved rock and hauled cement – tons and tons of cement. When new machinery arrived on the railroad several miles away, the tractors hauled them, intact, to the aqueduct. Wherever great bulk or weight was concerned, nothing seemed too much for these magnificent machines. They routinely hauled material across deep sand and easily climbed up steep grades.

Soon after the huge tractors demonstrated their value to the construction project, the company ordered twenty-five more of the machines, as well as seventy-eight specially designed Holt wagons. These machines often carried loads that weighed as much as fifty tons, and progress on the aqueduct construction increased dramatically.

The huge herd of mules, it should be noted, remained a very valuable resource in the construction of the aqueduct. Hauling less bulky equipment from one job site to another nearby site by mule proved to be more efficient than the tractors. The mules and the caterpillars, therefore, complimented one another.

11

WHILE MULHOLLAND TRIED to spend as much time as possible at the aqueduct job site, the reality was that other concerns of the company often kept him busy inside his office, which was located near the Plaza in downtown Los Angeles.

On one of those days, he sat in the plush chair behind his desk. This was not a happy occasion for him. The news that he had recently received caused him both sadness and disappointment, for he was a man of honor and high ethical standards. The task that lay before him created a sick and empty feeling within him.

A knock on the door caused the tension within him to rise. A moment later the door opened and Fred Eaton entered.

"What's up, Boss?" Fred asked good naturedly as he took a seat facing the desk.

Mulholland remained silent for a long moment as he stared directly at Eaton. He was not looking forward to this discussion, but he had it to do.

"Fred," he began at last, "I want to talk to you about that land you purchased up in Round Valley, on the Owens River north of the lake. You assured me that you had ceded all the water rights to the city of Los Angeles." He shrugged, then added, "In fact, you even said as much in an interview a few years ago with the *Los Angeles Express*."

"That's right, I did." Eaton replied. "And like I explained to the press, I retained the cattle, which was part of the deal in purchasing the ranch. That mountain pasture land is of little use except for grazing cattle."

"That's not what I'm concerned about!" Mulholland replied. It was clear he was perturbed. "You were also fully aware that a portion of that land, located on the Owens River, upstream from the Owens River Gorge, was to be used as a reservoir by the water company." Following another pause, he added, "And, of course, that included your so-called 'mountain pasture land.'"

"The Owens River Gorge was a natural reservoir for the large amount of water needed for the city of Los Angeles. And now, unfortunately, we can't use it. We'll have to find another storage place."

"Why can't we use it?"

"You know why! It's because you are demanding one million dollars from the city of Los Angeles for the land you purchased." As he stared at the man who had once been his boss when he first went to work for the water department, a sick feeling came over Mulholland as he added, "I am here to tell you that it is my recommendation that the city refuse to pay you for that land."

Eaton flushed with insolent anger. Staring at his boss, he asked, "And just where do you propose to find that reservoir?"

"I'll let that be my secret for the time being."

Eaton was seething. "Will that be all?" he asked.

"That's all."

"Should I tender my resignation?"

"That won't be necessary. You're still a valuable part of this project, and I don't want to lose you. At the same time, I want you to know where I stand on this issue."

Eaton glared coldly at his boss as he stood up to leave.

It saddened Mulholland as he realized that things would never be the same between him and Eaton again.

12

Once work actually began on the aqueduct I seldom saw Bill Mulholland, for he spent most of his time engrossed in attending to the myriad details relating to the construction of an aqueduct along much of the length of Jawbone Canyon, installing huge concrete pipes, six feet in diameter. Digging tunnels through sections of the Tehachapi Mountains was also a tremendous challenge. The aqueduct would, in time, come to be recognized as one of the greatest engineering feats in history.

Though I seldom came across Bill during these years, I read of his accomplishments almost daily in the local newspapers.

JAWBONE CANYON IS a dry, arid part of the Mojave Desert, set between the El Paso Mountains to the east and the Tehachapi Mountains to the west. The construction of the aqueduct ran from south of Owens Lake then southwest through Jawbone Canyon, to the eastern foothills of the Tehachapi range. It would eventually flow all the way, through mountains and canyons, to its destination in a spillway north of San Fernando, in Los Angeles County.

The miles of open trench that comprised much of the aqueduct in Jawbone Canyon was lined with concrete. In the regions where the terrain was too rugged for ditch digging, huge pipes, called inverted siphons, with a diameter wide enough to literally drive a car through, were employed. It was hard and tedious work. The Caterpillar tractors played an important part in minimizing much of the manual labor involved in this phase of the aqueduct construction.

Threats of sabotage had become fairly common. Several inhabitants of the Owens Valley towns, egged on by Emmett Hollister and others, made several attempts to blow up sections of the aqueduct. It became necessary to hire guards to protect the work sites. Among those hired was a man Mulholland met in Cantil. He was young and in need of employment. His name was Tony Harnischfeger. He lived with his common law wife. Tony seemed to be a competent sort, so the Boss took a chance and hired him. During the months that followed Tony proved to be competent in his job. The presence of these guards served to reduce the acts of sabotage, but not end them all together.

Perhaps the most difficult task was the digging of tunnels. It was a slow and physically challenging job and took a total of five years to dig one hundred forty-two tunnels, totaling forty-three miles, before the aqueduct was completed. Eighteen of those tunnels went through the Tehachapi Mountains.

The Elizabeth Tunnel at Lake Hughes, near the end of the aqueduct, was probably the most challenging dig. It was five miles in length and crossed the San Andreas fault. The tunnel workers actually set a world record by digging more than six hundred feet in one month. In the fall of 1913, eight years after work began, and the installation of more than fifteen thousand tons of steel, the aqueduct was completed.

This had been a major undertaking and would go down in history as one of the two greatest engineering feats in U.S. history – second only to the Panama Canal.

ON NOVEMBER FIFTH of that year a ceremony took place at the terminus of the aqueduct, where the water flowed into the Lower San Fernando Reservoir. A large crowd showed up for the big event. Though many of them were long-time residents of the area, they had only recently become citizens of Los Angeles. This was due primarily to a specific condition regarding the use of this water. That condition was that only residents and businesses within the city limits of Los Angeles would have access. This resulted in several towns and cities on the outskirts of Los Angeles becoming annexed, thus significantly increasing the size of the city, in both population and geography.

When William and Lillie Mulholland arrived at the ceremony, Bill was surprised by the large number of celebrants that showed up. His surprise was due to the fact that the ceremony was being held in a very sparsely populated site in a northern section of the San Fernando Valley.

Lillie stole a glance at her husband and frowned. Though he was known as a man of few words, she was aware that he had taken no time to prepare a speech, and he was, after all, the man of the hour.

"Oh, well," she sighed inwardly. "He knows what he is doing … always does."

During the course of the morning most of the big wigs in city government had an opportunity to speak from a large platform high above, causing the speakers to look down on the sizable crowd. For the most part the speeches were long and drawn out. Behind the speaker were several chairs on which the dignitaries sat. Finally, it was time for Mulholland, the man of the hour, to get up and deliver his address, and Lillie worriedly gazed at her husband as he made his way to the podium.

Looking out over the expectant crowd, his back to the huge pipes that were, at that moment, spilling water into the reservoir, he said, "Only water was needed to make this region a tremendously rich and productive empire, and now we have it." He paused only long enough to gesture behind him, toward the flowing water. He glanced in that direction briefly, then turned back toward the audience and announced, "There she is: take it." As he made his way back to his seat an explosion of cheers and applause followed him.

I am proud to say that I made it a point of attending this ceremony. It was a huge accomplishment for the city of Los Angeles. Water was truly becoming scarce. Though there were numerous citrus groves within the city, the limited amount of water allotted to the growth of these trees was insufficient to produce good fruit. The oranges, lemons and such that were harvested were tasteless, and the meat was dry. The farmers were unable to sell their products. It was a foregone conclusion that this aqueduct, bringing water from the Owens Valley, would be a Godsend for the fruit growers in Los Angeles.

As I sat in the audience and listened to Bill's words, I thought back to my friend, Jim Boyer. He was the deputy sheriff Henry Mitchell assigned to escort Bill and Hugh to where the Deakers family lived when they first arrived in Los Angeles. Jim was the one who related to Bill and Hugh the need for more water in the area in order for the city to grow. While Bill didn't give it much thought at the time, Jim's words remained in the back of his mind. I wish Jim were here today, but sadly, he has passed on. He was, after all, the one who planted the seed that grew into what we came here to celebrate.

13

THE YEAR FOLLOWING the completion of the aqueduct another major event occurred that would, in time, have a huge impact on the growth of Los Angeles. The man who spearheaded this event was movie director Cecil B. DeMille.

Motion pictures were in their infancy, and the vast majority were shot in the east, particularly New York and New Jersey. Because of frequent bad weather these movies were shot inside studios, some of which were nothing more than large wood-framed structures walled in by tar paper. It was pitch dark inside so the studio could provide the exact amount of artificial lighting needed to film the production. Of course, this limited the scope of the story the movie could provide, and most of the features were one-or-two reelers that tried to tell a story in less than twenty minutes.

DeMille dreamed of spectacular productions, filmed both indoors and out in wide expanses, and one reelers were not sufficient for him to tell a story. His two partners, Jesse Lasky and Samuel Goldwyn, agreed with DeMille, so they made plans to move the studio west.

Their first destination was Flagstaff, Arizona. With high mountains in the background, it was a perfect setting for outdoor shots. When the train pulled in at the station it was pouring down rain. Two days later it was still raining.

Frustrated, the three partners decided to move farther west. A few days later they were in sunny California.

Shortly after their arrival they set up shop in an area of Los Angeles called Hollywood. The three partners called their business Lasky Film Company. In that same year they produced a six reeler, called *The Squaw Man*, co-directed by Cecil B. DeMille. The picture was a huge success, and soon other movie companies migrated west to take advantage of the mild weather and the spectacular outdoor scenery.

It was not long before an army of actors, technicians, screen writers and others seeking employment in the movie industry migrated to Hollywood. Lasky Film Company would eventually evolve into Paramount Pictures. That same year German immigrant Carl Laemmle purchased the large Taylor Ranch near Hollywood and started Universal Studios. Practically from the beginning the studio was open to the public. Since the movies had no sound, Laemmle encouraged the fans to watch films being made and laugh, cry and applaud as much as they pleased. The noise did not interfere with production. The Hollywood motion picture industry was off and running. The population boomed, and the demand for more water increased exponentially.

UPON COMPLETION OF the aqueduct, William Mulholland turned his attention to the site for a large reservoir designed to hold a great quantity of water, to be used in the event an unforeseen shortage of water occurred. This reservoir would have sufficient water to supply Los Angeles until the water shortage issue was resolved.

This had been one of the purposes of the site north of Bishop for a proposed reservoir in Owens Gorge, a ten-mile-long steep canyon that was ideal for water storage. Another purpose was to supply water for farmers in Owens Valley. It had been the bone of contention between Mulholland and Eaton. Eaton had misrepresented himself to the residents of Owens Valley, inferring that he was a representative of the federal government, contending that water storage in Owens Gorge would also be used to assist farmers in times of drought. Many farmers donated portions of their land for the water project. Meanwhile, Fred Eaton was absorbing thousands of acres for his own personal use. When the time was right, in his judgement, he offered to sell a portion of his land to the city of Los Angeles for one million dollars – considerably more than what he had paid for it. Some of this land was that which had been donated by farmers in Owens Valley. As a result, the Owens Gorge plan was discontinued, and Mulholland was searching for another major site to store a very large quantity of water. Sadly, the new reservoir would not be beneficial to the people of Owens Valley, but it would serve the people of Los Angeles in the event of drought.

The initial site that Mulholland looked at was in Big Tujunga Canyon, near Sunland, in the northeast part of the San Fernando Valley.

Unfortunately, the asking price for the land was excessively high. In the end, he selected a canyon that was, in part, federally owned. The privately owned portions of San Francisquito Canyon were sold to the city at reasonable prices.

San Francisquito Canyon was a fairly narrow cut between two ranges of hills running from east and west for six miles, eventually terminating at the Santa Clara River. At one time it had been a pass, or short cut, on journeys between Los Angeles and San Joaquin Valley. The east end of the canyon rose upward between the two sides, so little work would be needed to contain a rather deep storage of water. Four miles west, into the canyon, was where Mulholland had selected as the preferred site for the dam. This site would occupy much of his attention over the next several years.

IN LATE APRIL 1915, tragedy struck once again in the Mulholland family. On the twenty-eighth of that month William's beloved wife, Lillie, passed away following a brief illness. She was only forty-seven years old.

With the exception of Ruth, all of his children were grown, but none of them were married. Rose Ellen, the oldest, assumed the duties of running the house. William, consistent with his nature, buried himself in his work, which resumed two days after the funeral.

A month after the death of Lillie Mulholland the city of Los Angeles annexed major portions of San Fernando Valley. The primary impetus of the annexation was access to the water flowing from Owens Lake. The cities of Burbank, Lankershim, Owensmouth and the town of San Fernando, along with Rancho El Scorpion chose not to be annexed. But the reality of the water shortage, and the fact that the city was quite serious about the use of the water being restricted to residents and businesses of Los Angeles, Owensmouth would be annexed in 1917, followed by West Lankershim in 1919, then the rest of Lankershim in 1923. Other areas of the Valley would follow in time. The towns of Burbank and San Fernando remained independent, as did most of Rancho El Scorpion. By 1924 most of the two hundred sixty square miles of the San Fernando Valley were officially part of the city of Los Angeles.

GEORGE THORNTON EDWARDS arrived in Los Angeles in 1916, after graduating from a prestigious private school a year earlier. Having come from an affluent family in Maine, it must have come as a shock to them when he announced his intention of going to Hollywood and becoming a movie actor.

Ever the optimist, Thornton, as he preferred being called, knocked on the doors at studios until one decided to take a chance on this good-looking, darkish complected young man who did not know the meaning of giving up. Before the year was out he got roles in two movies, *Eye of the night*, and *Lieutenant Danny, U.S.A.* He was on his way.

Though he seldom, if ever, played a lead role, he usually had a significant part among the supporting cast. His easygoing sense of humor endeared him to the actors, directors and technicians alike.

Thornton had been in Hollywood only a matter of months before he met the woman of his dreams. Her name was Ethel Hopper, a twenty-one-year-old from New York, whose pretty, clean-cut looks almost immediately landed her a place among Mack Sennett's Bathing Beauties. These movies were short – usually one or two reelers, and Ethel would appear in several of them between 1916 and the early 1920s. Because she was consistently busy, Ethel's salary was higher than that of her husband. Unlike most of his contemporaries, Thornton did not allow his ego to get the better of him. He loved his wife, and he was quite proud of her budding success. They had both vowed that their marriage would be for life. Seventy years later, their love for one another, as well as their marriage vows, would be as strong as ever. In 1918, Ethel gave birth to a son. They named him George Thornton Edwards, Jr.

By 1921 Thornton had appeared in twenty-seven movies, but he was not happy. They were always supporting roles, generally of no more than a few days' work. During these early days of film making, actors were paid a small salary only for the days they worked. For an actor in a supporting role, the total the job might require only one- or two-days' work. The meager income, therefore, was simply not enough to support a family. After much discussion, he and Ethel decided to leave the movie business and seek other employment.

In 1922, Thornton was sworn in as a motorcycle officer for the city of Santa Paula, California. Eighteen years later he would return to the movie business. These would be talkies, and, in many cases, his part would be larger, and the salary would be a great deal more than what he was making as a silent screen actor.

It was during the period between his silent and talking movie days, however, that an incident occurred that would bring him into the greatest public role of his life – not in Hollywood, but in the real world of William Mulholland.

WILLIAM S. HART was another easterner who traveled to Hollywood in search of fame in movies. Unlike Thornton Edwards, however, Hart was a professional actor, having recently come from the Broadway stage. One of his roles was that of Masala, in the stage production of *Ben Hur*. He was also no stranger to Shakespearian roles.

Hart was fifty years old when he made his screen debut, and almost immediately he was a leading man. Much of his childhood had been spent in the West, accompanying his father to the Dakotas. He became acquainted with various Indian tribes and even spoke their language. He loved the West and was quite knowledgeable about its history.

Along with Tom Mix and Harry Carey, Hart's Western movies were immediate hits, filling the theaters across the country with adults and children alike. He quickly counted such luminaries as Will Rogers, Charley Chaplin, Douglas Fairbanks and Mary Pickford among his closest friends.

Though the part he would later play in the life of William Mulholland was not as large as the role that would be played by Thornton Edwards, it is certainly worth mentioning.

ON MAY 11, 1918, William Mulholland's brother, Hugh, passed away. Cancer took him at the age of sixty.

When the brothers first arrived in Los Angeles in 1877, Hugh had been unimpressed with the town, and he soon departed in search of a better life elsewhere. Over the years William and Hugh stayed in touch with one another. On at least one occasion William took a short break from his work at the water company to join Hugh in Washington, purportedly to "study the rivers." In reality, William would have found any excuse to spend time with his brother.

In later years Hugh did, in fact, return to Los Angeles, and that is where he died. The wayward brother left behind his wife, Mahala Alice, and a number of children.

True to his nature, the day following the burial of his brother, William Mulholland was back at work.

TUESDAY
March 13, 1928

6:20 A.M.

FRANK KIENAST AND his son, Jeff, arrived at the sheriff's office in Independence following their drive from the ranch outside of Bishop. Sitting at a desk behind the front counter was a deputy sheriff. Looking up at the two men, he arose and moved toward them.

"Good morning, Mr. Kienast," the deputy greeted with a smile. "What can I do for you this early in the morning?"

"Good morning, Ernest. We were wondering if you could get in touch with the sheriff's office down in Newhall – in Los Angeles County."

The deputy's smile faded. "Is this about the dam collapse down there?"

Frank turned toward his son, who was staring back at his father. He was about to blurt out an affirmative to the question, but some inner voice told him to say nothing. "What dam collapse?" he asked innocently.

"Just past midnight last night they had a major dam collapse and a lot of people have been killed."

Frank had to think fast. "Well, I'm not going to bother them with my petty concerns. Sounds like they have their hands full." Patting his hand on the counter, he added, "I'll just check back with them later." Before turning to leave, Frank added, "Be seeing you, Ernest."

As the two turned to leave, the deputy shrugged and returned to his desk.

They had driven two miles before Jeff managed to gather the words to ask the question that was burning within both of them.

"Dad, do you think Uncle Emmett was responsible for the dam break?"

"I don't know, son. You yourself said he never actually mentioned destroying the dam." Frank was silent for a moment before adding, "Just the same I can't help but wonder why in blazes he would want you to fly him over it."

"That's the way I feel." Jeff agreed before adding, "It just doesn't make sense."

They were half-way into their forty-one-mile drive to Bishop when Jeff asked, "Would you mind if we stop by the Lundstrums on our way home?"

"The Lundstrums?" Frank asked. "Jeff, it's still rather early to be calling on folks."

"It'll be close to eight o'clock when we get there. Besides, the Lundstrums are early risers." There was silence for the better part of a minute before Jeff added, "I need to see Angela. It's important to me."

Frank Kienast and Jim Lundstrum had been friends since before Jeff and Angela were born. Since Anna's passing, however, their social visits had not been as frequent."

Breathing a sigh, Frank said, "We'll stop by for a minute or so, then we need to get back to the ranch."

An hour later Frank was sitting at the kitchen table with Jim and Martha. He had politely refused their offer of breakfast but did accept a cup of coffee. Jeff and Angela, meanwhile, had stepped outside so they could talk in private. Jeff related the news to her about the dam collapse but mentioned nothing about his uncle's possible involvement.

With shoulder-length auburn hair and deep hazel eyes and an attractive figure, Angela could have had her pick of the boys at Bishop High School, yet she shunned them in favor of spending her time with Jeff. While she was away at college, the two corresponded with one another at least once a week.

Jeff could not remember exactly when he began to fall in love with her, for they had been best friends all of their lives. They were often seen at social gatherings together, and occasionally the young couple attended a movie in Bishop. Jeff had developed into a nice-looking young man, though not as strikingly attractive to women as Angela was to men. But if someone asked who his best friend was, he would not hesitate to say it was Angela.

"Angie, I need to go there to see if there is any way I can help – maybe airlift someone somewhere. If nothing else I can help with rescue and recovery. I'm sure they'll be needing all the help they can get." Pausing long enough to breathe a sigh, he added, "What I'd like to know is: would you be willing to fly down there with me?"

The question caught Angela off guard. It was not a matter of flying, for she had flown with Jeff on numerous occasions, but not this far – not as far as Los Angeles.

Angela offered a reluctant frown. "I don't know, Jeff." She hesitated briefly before adding, "I don't think my parents would approve of me going."

"Why not? You've flown with me numerous times."

"It's not the flying. It's what we are going down there to do." When Jeff made no immediate reply, she continued, "It's what we'll be seeing – all the devastation and … and death." Her frown remained as she added, "I just don't know."

Fifteen minutes later Frank and Jeff were back on the road heading to the ranch. The disappointment was evident on Jeff's face.

"What's wrong, son?" Frank asked. "Did something happen between you and Angela?"

"No. Not really." He stared out the window, at the countryside before adding, "I just asked her to join me on a flight down to the dam area. She said no."

"The dam area! Why would you want to do that?" The announcement caught Frank off guard, and he had to fight off the anger and disappointment building inside of him. "You just got back from a two-day trip down there, and I might add that you had me worried sick about you!"

"I apologize for that Dad, I'm truly sorry. But the reality is, I'm almost twenty-four years old. I am an experienced pilot and have my own plane. I'm sure they can use me." He paused as another thought occurred to him. "Why don't you come with me, Dad?"

"You know better than that!" Frank replied, more forcefully than he intended. "You know how I feel about those contraptions."

Jeff regretted having offered the suggestion. It was no secret that his dad had a fear of flying. In Jeff's eyes, his dad was every bit a man. He was tough and willing to face almost anything. But he had a deathly fear of flying.

"Besides," Frank continued, "We have a shipment of hay arriving sometime today."

"Dad, you have a foreman who can handle that," Jeff objected.

Ignoring his son's reply, Frank added, "And it won't be long before the hands will be turning out for branding. I'm going to need your help. You're always there for the branding."

Jeff was quite aware that spring was around the corner, and that was when ranch activities began to pick up. But it was still cool, and spring would not officially be here for another week or so. That was when the branding would begin.

Breathing a deep sigh, Jeff replied, "I'll be home in time for the branding."

It was primarily a horse ranch, but cattle were also raised on a smaller scale. Shipping was restricted to slaughter houses within the state of California. It helped to finance the operation of the ranch, but horse breeding was the primary source of income.

He was well aware that he would, in time, take over the business of running the ranch, but at the moment he was just a paid employee. His presence was not that critical, and at the moment he felt compelled to make this trip.

As soon as they arrived home Jeff went directly to the hangar to make a safety check of his plane, as he did prior to every flight. A few years earlier he had an underground gasoline tank installed. It was used for machinery on the ranch, as well as for fueling the plane. After the safety checks and refueling, Jeff left the plane parked at the head of the runway, then went to the house to grab a mid-morning snack to eat before taking off.

Upon entering the kitchen, he was pleasantly surprised to see Angela sitting at the table with his dad.

"Angie! What are you doing here? I thought you said…"

"I know what I said," she replied with a smile. "I talked over what you said with my parents and, surprisingly, they thought it was a Christian thing to do. So, Dad drove me out here and," she paused briefly with a grin, "here I am." She lifted a small bag from the floor and added, "I know there's little room for extra items, but I thought a change of clothes would be all right."

"Good idea. We'll be ok with a few small items. In fact, I'll be taking a small bag with me, as well." He was pleased to see that she was wearing denim pants and a heavy flannel shirt. It was obvious that she was prepared to get dirty if need be.

Turning his attention to his dad, he said, "We'll be leaving in a few minutes. I intend to make a stop in Mojave to refuel, then continue over toward Newhall."

"Where will you land once you get to Newhall?" Frank asked.

"I've heard there are a few ranches in the area that use planes in their work, and they have their own private airstrips." Shrugging his shoulders, Jeff added, "We'll take a chance that we can keep the plane there. If not, I'm sure they'll have a suggestion as to where we can find a nearby runway."

"Are you sure?" A look of concern appeared on his father's face.

Jeff offered a smile. "Flyers are a close-knit group. We tend to take care of our own. Every pilot realizes that, at one time or another, it might be his turn to ask a favor."

"How long do you expect to be gone?" his dad wanted to know.

"I'm guessing about a week, maybe ten days." When his father made no reply, Jeff added, "I'll try to send you a telegram tomorrow with more information. I'll also include the phone number of the sheriff's station in Newhall. If you need to get in touch with me, I'm sure they will know how to find me."

"I'll send a wire to my folks as well," Angela added.

A few minutes later Frank Kienast stood outside the back door and watched as the Curtiss Jenny lifted off the ground and headed south, toward Mojave.

IV:
PRELUDE TO
DISASTER
1922-1928

14

THORNTON AND ETHEL both fell in love with Santa Paula at first sight. The town nestled comfortably among rolling hills where orange groves and lemon groves dotted the landscape, and the rich green leaves of avocado trees decorated the hillsides. Running along the edge of town was the Santa Clara River, its banks sloped gently down to a slow-running stream of water. The fishing was good and fit in naturally with the quiet and peaceful atmosphere of Santa Paula.

In the eyes of Thornton and Ethel, this was the ideal town in which to raise their son, who was now four years old. They were a happy family, and so far as they both were concerned, this was where they would spend their lives.

Thornton was sworn in as a member of the Santa Paula Police Department and assigned as a motorcycle officer. It was not long before Officer Edwards was known throughout the area. His friendly disposition, as well as his outgoing personality and sense of humor, endeared him to the community. Though he strictly enforced the law, he did so in a friendly, respectful manner, and there was seldom any occasions for resentment.

IN OWENS VALLEY discontent was growing. The Los Angeles Water Company was in the process of slowly buying up property in the region. The drying up of ground water was having a huge negative impact on the farmers in the area. Their once fertile land appeared to be on the throes of death.

It was true that, each spring, the melted snow from the Sierras replenished the water supply – to an extent. By mid-summer, however, much of the water was lost, and the long period between summer and the following spring brought desperation for the people who lived and worked in Owens Valley.

An argument from the water company was that, once the reservoirs in and around Los Angeles were filled, ensuring Los Angeles of water during the dry months, the river should maintain a steady flow that would be less than what the Owens River provided. This, however, was yet to be the case.

IN 1923 A meeting was called near Lone Pine by Emmett Hollister. It took place outside of town, amid a boulder strewn section of the Alabama Hills. Only twelve people showed up – all men. It was a rowdy group who tended to lean toward violence as a counteraction to the "theft" of their water.

Hollister was a bitter man. At the age of twenty-three he had married the person he thought was the woman of his dreams. The marriage, however, was short-lived. Within a year she deserted him for parts unknown. His natural tendency toward bitterness was fed by the broken marriage. And by now, at the age of forty-seven, it had evolved into a resentment of life in general.

Emmett Hollister was also a man of contradiction. Though he had a proclivity toward obtaining things without working for them, of late he had thoughts of becoming a preacher. It came about when someone convinced him that there was money to be made in hawking his version of the Word of God. The fact that he was gifted with a convincing way with words, much like a door-to-door salesman, would help in this endeavor.

This was his mind set when he called the meeting in the Alabama Hills. His "congregation" consisted of an assortment of thugs who tended to gravitate toward the likes of Emmett Hollister. He started the meeting with a prayer, then went into a sermon that quickly declined into a tirade about William Mulholland and the sin of stealing what was rightfully the property of the citizens of Owens Valley.

"In Mulholland's service to Satan," he preached, "his actions, as well as the actions of the powers that be in Los Angeles, have lured the godless heads of the moving picture industry. Scantily-clad women parading around on the screen – enticing adults and children alike to sin. The thousands of sinful people in this business are now firmly embedded throughout the city that should, rightfully, be called Babylon. It is common practice for movie actors and actresses to go from one spouse to another searching for erotic pleasure. Movie-goers watch this behavior and try to copy it. The city's population is growing and becoming more sinful by the day, and the demand for water will suck Owens Valley dry in their attempt to satisfy this unquenchable thirst in Babylon."

His tirade succeeded in working up the "congregation." Following the sermon, they set about making plans to sabotage the aqueduct somewhere south of Olancha. A few weeks after this act was carried out, another small section of the aqueduct was blown up in Jawbone Canyon. In both cases the damage was minimal. Water company workers quickly made repairs, but the occurrences did send a message to Mulholland that other acts of sabotage were inevitable.

EMMETT HOLLISTER'S PREACHING ambitions were short-lived. He had neither the scriptural knowledge nor the true calling to pursue this line of work. Those who were honest believers quickly saw through his attempts to build a congregation for personal financial gain, and soon the entire community turned their backs on him, labeling him a kook and a fraud. Instead of becoming hurt by their rejection of him, Hollister became angry and resentful, and some day he would show these pious sheep just how much of a man he was. He had only to bide his time.

IN JULY 1924 Emmett's sister, Anna Kienast, passed away of a brain tumor. She was forty-three years old. Emmett was devastated by her passing, for, aside from his nephew, Jeff Kienast, she had been his only known blood relative.

At the funeral Emmett sat in the last pew of the church. When Frank Kienast saw him he approached his brother-in-law and invited him to join him and Jeff in the front row. Emmett stared at Frank for several seconds, then turned his head away. Frank heaved an audible sigh, then returned to the front of the church. In the months and years that followed there was little contact between Frank Kienast and his brother-in-law.

15

HARVEY VAN NORMAN was a handsome young man of twenty-nine when he went to work for the water company. Mulholland recognized the younger man's talents as an engineer, as well as his ethical work standards, and, over the next ten years he would advance in the company to become one of its top executives.

In 1924, while Mulholland was in Arizona examining the prospects of eventually drawing additional water from the Colorado River, Van Norman was dispatched to Owens Valley to allay some concerns among the citizenry about the amount of water being taken from the Owens River by Los Angeles.

When he arrived, Van Norman became aware that the situation was worse than he feared. The entire valley was up in arms about the city's usurpation – not only of the water, but of the acquisition of great tracts of land in the vicinity of the Owens River.

In spite of several meetings he attended with town officials, he was unable to resolve any of their complaints. He returned to Los Angeles, deeply concerned that the people were on the verge of rebelling against the Los Angeles Water Company.

A WEEK OR SO following Van Norman's failed attempts to reach a peaceful solution to their concerns, over one hundred citizens of Inyo County seized a section of the aqueduct and opened the Alabama gates four miles north of Lone Pine. Emmett Hollister tried to join the group in an attempt to eventually take over its leadership. At this time, however, the community wanted no part of his "shenanigans", as one woman put it, so he departed angrily, and had nothing more to do with the take-over.

Ranchers, farmers and townspeople joined together for the purpose of sending a message to William Mulholland. During the five-day siege of the aqueduct the number of participants grew. Women in the community provided picnic-style meals to feed the men who guarded the open gate. Crowds from outlying areas joined the group, and the local sheriff requested law enforcement assistance from the governor, who promptly denied the request. In his reply the governor pointed out that it was strange that the parties seeking law enforcement assistance were the aggressors in the matter, while the parties being attacked had not requested any help. The matter should be handled in the courts.

Meanwhile, Tom Mix, perhaps the most popular western actor at the time, was filming a movie in the nearby Alabama Hills. Not one to pass up an opportunity to gain publicity, he rode his famous horse, Tony, up to the flood gates where the crowd had gathered. He made no speeches, for he really had nothing to say. His only purpose was to gain exposure from the large gathering of local townsfolk.

In the eyes of most of the attendees, however, the very presence of this Hollywood celebrity was proof that he was there to lend support to their cause. Nevertheless, a month later Tom Mix showed up at the opening ceremony of the Mulholland Highway, where Bill Mulholland was the honoree. The fact of the matter was that his attendance at these opposing events had nothing to do with politics, but, rather, exposure to a large, friendly crowd. Tom Mix was a natural-born showman.

Finally, after four days, the gate was shut off by the protesters, conceding that the matter should go to court. The city of Los Angeles filed a brief in court alleging that damages amounted to fifteen thousand dollars for each day they allowed water to flow out of the aqueduct. The conflict was eventually resolved, but not to the satisfaction of all the parties involved.

WHILE THE CONFLICT raged in Owens Valley, workers began construction of the St. Francis Dam in San Francisquito Canyon. Upon completion, the face of the dam would rise one hundred eighty feet above the streambed, the equivalent height of an eighteen-story building. It would contain thirty-thousand-acre feet, or twelve billion gallons, of water. Completion of the dam was a priority for Mulholland, so most of the emphasis was on completing the project in as short a time as possible.

As construction of the dam was a priority, the situation in Owens Valley continued to fester. The same year construction of the dam began, Owens Lake dried up. This was due, primarily, to the diversion of the river away from the lake. While there was still plenty of water flowing in the river, the dry lake was a visual symbol to those who lived in the area that Los Angeles was stealing their water. The powers that be in the valley, however, were quite aware that they were being paid generously for the precious commodity.

While the dam was under construction, various factions from Owens Valley continued to carry out acts of sabotage. Most of the attempts to destroy the aqueduct took place in or near Inyo County, although there were some attempts to destroy sections in or around the tunnels. One incident took place at what was called the No Name Tunnel. Vandals floated two cases of blasting gelatin down the No Name siphon. Only one of the cases exploded, but it was enough to blow a large hole in the metal wall of the siphon, causing serious damage.

These acts of sabotage, along with claims against Owens Valley property that was legally purchased by the city of Los Angeles, ended up doing significant financial damage to the Inyo County residents – as well as some prominent businesses. One of those businesses was the Inyo County Bank. This came about after the owners, who were active participants in the property damage to aqueduct-related property, were charged with embezzlement. The closing of the bank left many citizens of the area, who had no active interest in the water war with Los Angeles, penniless. Life savings were wiped out. This, for the most part, ended the popularity of local aqueduct vandals. Acts of sabotage were greatly reduced.

ON MARCH 12, 1926, the St. Francis Dam was completed. It would take some time for the aqueduct to deliver such a great quantity of water, but eventually the reservoir would be full. At the inner wall of the dam the water depth was one hundred eighty feet to the floor. The canyon behind the wall was not particularly wide, nor was it as deep as it was at the base of the dam, but the canyon that made up the reservoir was four miles long. When full, the reservoir would hold a massive quantity of water.

Two years later, almost to the date, the dam would collapse, and all those billions of gallons of water would come crashing down on an unsuspecting populace. In terms of lives lost, it would be the largest man-made disaster in California history.

TUESDAY
March 13, 1928

1:15 A.M.

MERLE CLINTON DROVE the five-year-old Ford Model T at top speed north along the highway that separated Lancaster from Mojave, a distance of thirty miles. The most he could get out of the car was forty miles per hour. No matter how he pushed down on the gas lever, which was attached to the steering column, the car could not muster any more speed.

Twenty-five minutes earlier he had been drinking coffee in a café in Lancaster when a deputy sheriff entered, a concerned expression on his face. He was wearing a loose-fitting suit with a badge pinned to the lapel. As the deputy took a seat at the counter he was greeted by the waiter, who seemed to know him.

"Morning Jim," the waiter greeted. "Why the long face?"

"You haven't heard?" the deputy asked. "Oh, no. I guess you wouldn't have heard yet, since the lines have been down near Newhall."

"Heard what?" the waiter prompted.

"That dam over in Francisquito Canyon." He paused briefly, then added, "It busted, and is flooding the whole area for miles around." Following another pause, the deputy shook his head sadly. "They're saying hundreds of folks have drowned."

A full minute passed before Merle rose from his seat, paid for his coffee and left the café. And now he was rushing to the motor court in Mojave to let Hollister know that somebody had beaten them to the dam.

Merle had been in Lancaster since late afternoon to purchase some boxes of Garrett Snuff. He had an addiction to the snuff but had failed to bring along a sufficient supply to last for more than a few days. He had attempted to purchase several boxes in Mojave but could not find a store that sold it. Someone suggested he drive to Lancaster. There were several stores in the larger community that sold the snuff.

He had little trouble finding it, but before starting back to the motor court he decided to have a few beers in a local speakeasy. Three hours later he walked, somewhat unsteadily, out of the bar and made it to the café, where he began guzzling coffee in an effort to become sober enough to make the drive back to Lancaster. He had become alarmed when the deputy sheriff entered the café, but the lawman was obviously too preoccupied with news of the dam to recognize a drunk when he saw one.

The next twenty minutes seemed to add to the anxiety that Merle was experiencing, but eventually he stopped the car in front of the motel. Moving hurriedly to the door where Hollister and his other companion, Albert Slocumb, were sleeping. Merle banged on the door until Hollister opened it.

"What are you trying to do? Wake up everyone in the motor court?" Hollister asked angrily.

Merle started to comment that there were no other visitors in the court but refrained from further angering his boss. Inside the room Merle excitedly related the news about the dam.

"Are you sure it's the same dam?" Hollister wanted to know.

"Well, the cop said it was the dam in Francisquito Canyon."

For the better part of a minute the room was quiet, then a slow smile appeared on Hollister's face. "Well now," he began, "Looks like our job has been done for us. We might as well head back home."

"What are we gonna do with all this dynamite?" Albert Slocumb wanted to know. "We gotta get rid of it somehow." Following a brief pause, Slocumb continued. "On our way home maybe we could take a detour into Jawbone Canyon and do some damage to the aqueduct."

"No. That would be pushing our luck," Hollister replied. "Because of the dam collapse everyone involved with Mulholland is on the alert." Following a prolonged silence, Hollister snapped his fingers. "I've got it! On our drive back we can take a detour into Red Rock Canyon. It's on the way to Independence. Inside the canyon we'll find a place to bury the stuff – sticks, fuses, boxes and all! We'll bury it deep, then find a small boulder to roll over it."

The room at the motor court had been paid for in advance, so there was no reason to notify the manager of their departure. Twenty minutes later they were on the highway heading north. In less than an hour they would be inside Red Rock Canyon.

V:
DAMBREAK!
March 12 and 13, 1928

16

TONY HARNISCHFEGER SAT in a chair he had brought from the kitchen to the front porch of his small cottage. Leaning back in the chair until its upper back rested against the wall, he took a drag on his cigarette and contemplated the events of this day. It began with the arrival of William Mulholland and Harvey Van Norman. They had responded to his request to examine what he believed was a sure sign that the dam was failing to hold the water as it should.

It was Van Norman who had descended to the lower part of the dam to examine that about which Tony had been concerned, then returned to the place where he and Mulholland were standing. He announced that there was slight leakage, but, since the water was free of dam residue there was no immediate need to take any action at this time. Tony liked Mr. Van Norman. He always treated him with respect, so the dam keeper took him at his word.

Mulholland, on the other hand, was always harsh and critical of everything the dam keeper did, and Tony was still sulking from how the chief had talked to him that morning. He thought of resigning his post and taking his woman and child away. He shouldn't have any trouble finding a job someplace else.

The front door opened, and Leona Johnson stepped onto the porch. She was wearing a heavy sweater and holding a jacket in her hand that she offered to Tony.

"It's pretty chilly. Thought you might want to put this on," Leona said as she handed the jacket to Tony.

He eased the chair to an upright position and stood up to put on the jacket. "It's been gloomy and cold all day," he said, a note of sadness in his voice. "I'm thinking of getting out of here – find a job someplace else." He breathed a heavy sigh then added, "And if I never see another dam again it'll be too soon."

Leona offered an indifferent shrug. "Why don't we take a walk?" she suggested.

"What time is it?" he asked.

"It's a little past eleven."

Tony glanced toward the cottage, and Leona read his mind. "Coder is sound asleep," she replied, nodding toward the cottage where Tony's seven-year-old son slept.

"Where would you like to go?" He asked.

Leona shrugged. "Why don't we just walk up to the dam?"

"Why the dam?"

"Oh, I don't know." She replied, then added, "It's just a destination. It's a quarter mile away, so if we go there and back we will have walked half a mile."

Tony shrugged, then the two of them moved in that direction. The cottage sat in the belly of the canyon. It seemed an odd place to build it, and its location had been a source of concern for Tony – so much so that he had carved steps on the side of the canyon beside the cottage, hoping that it would be an escape route in case the dam broke. It was a futile gesture, for he realized that, in the event the dam ever collapsed the flood would be on them in a matter of seconds.

As they moved along the canyon floor Tony became suddenly aware that the ground beside the concrete-lined runoff ditch was wet. "It hasn't rained today, has it?"

Leona shrugged. "Not that I recall." She paused briefly before adding, "The sky has been gloomy all day, but I can't actually say if it has rained. Why do you ask?"

"Because the ground is wet. I'm afraid its coming from the dam."

"What should we do?" Leona asked, a note of concern in her voice.

"Nothing now, but I plan to call Mulholland's office first thing tomorrow and tell him about it." He frowned doubtfully. "Not that it'll do any good."

Upon reaching the center of the dam at its base Tony did what he always did – he stared up in wonder. The size of the structure never failed to amaze him. It was like standing on a sidewalk and staring up the side of an eighteen-story building. The curved walkway atop the structure measured seven hundred feet from one side of the canyon to the other. Behind the wall was twelve billion gallons of water pushing to get out. The dam had been built two thousand feet above sea level, and the natural flow of water was downhill, so there was a constant pressure against the wall of the dam. The water constantly pushed to flow downstream.

While Tony stared upward in nervous wonder, Leona strolled toward the east side of the structure. When she reached the end of the massive wall she began climbing up the bank toward the road that ran along the side of the reservoir toward Power House Station One, which sat back from the reservoir. She had only gone a few steps when she heard the engine sound of a motorcycle. It was moving along the dirt road atop the rim of the canyon. She saw the headlight beams as the motorcycle moved in front of her. She was too far down the side of the canyon for him to see her.

When the light faded as the motorcycle continued north, past the dam, Leona shrugged then turned and began descending toward the canyon floor. As she turned to walk back to where Tony was standing she heard an enormously loud sound, much like a booming clap of thunder. A second later the face of the dam seemed to explode, and a thunderous roar accompanied a massive wall of water. Tony vanished instantly. Leona, as if in a trance, turned back and began clawing her way up the bank, but it was a futile effort, for a large section of the dam collapsed near her and she was inundated by pieces of concrete, followed by a mountain of water. While she was struggling with her last gasp of breath a wall of water several stories high fell upon the tiny cottage. Young Coder never woke up.

A FEW MINUTES before the break in the dam Ace Hopewell rode his motorcycle along the narrow dirt road atop the eastern side of the canyon, enroute to Powerhouse Number One. It was an eerie night, with the moon hidden behind thick clouds. Shortly after passing the dam, Hopewell heard a rumbling sound behind him, but thought little of it. A moment later the sound of something like an explosion startled him. It had come from behind. He feared that it had been the dam breaking, but there was nothing he could do but continue on his ride to Power House Number One, near the northeast end of the reservoir. A few minutes later he arrived at his destination, where he received the news that the dam had failed.

PARALLELING FRANCISQUITO CANYON to the west was the Carey Ranch and Trading Post, owned by Harry Carey, the western movie star. It was a working ranch. The ranch employees were quite familiar with the dam, and some were concerned about its stability. While the ranch was separated by the west wall of the canyon, its height was only a minor barrier to the onrush of such a great amount of water. As the gargantuan wall of liquid, mud and concrete slammed against the west wall of the canyon much of the overflow rolled over the wall and created its own flood toward the Carey Ranch.

Adjacent to the Carey ranch, and nearest the canyon, was Chester Smith's ranch. The massive amount of water that went over the west wall of the canyon spilled onto the land that was owned by Smith, creating a huge flood of its own.

A young couple, who had started to work at the ranch only that morning, were asleep down in the employees' house, near the creek. Mr. and Mrs. Nichols, who were the employees vacating the ranch the following morning, were allowed to sleep in the ranch house. Chester Smith, for this night only, decided to sleep in the barn. He had also decided to leave the barn door open. Just as he was about to fall asleep he was awakened by a barking dog. Accompanying the dog's bark, was another sound. It took but a moment for him to realize that it was the roar of rushing water. For days he had been concerned by what Tony Harnischfeger had recently told him about the instability of the dam. The dam keeper had commented that it was unsafe and was likely to collapse at any time.

Smith, now fully awake, got up and rushed out of the barn. There was no time to warn the new employees, so he started running toward the main house to awaken Mr. and Mrs. Nichols. He was also running in the direction of the roaring sound. Smith started shouting as he ran, and the Nichols awoke and quickly ran out of the house, barefoot and only half dressed. The three of them made it to higher ground in the nick of time – cold and shivering, but alive.

INSIDE THE CANYON, near the road, James Erratchuo and his wife lived in a small house beside the road. He was awakened by a sound that he, at first, thought was a truck rumbling along the road. The sound had also awakened his wife, who joined her husband in the front room. The house began to shake violently, then gave a sudden jerk. James attempted to open the front door, but it would not open. This was followed by another shift of the walls. He grabbed his wife by the arm, lifted a leg and gave the door a powerful kick. The door opened upon them by a wall of water that pushed in upon them. The couple fell backward in the onrush, and James lost his grip on his wife's hand and felt her slip away from him. Moments later the rush of water passed, leaving the young man lying amid the rubble of his house. He began to frantically search for his wife, but she was nowhere to be found. James would survive, but his wife was lost in the flood, never to be seen again.

A MILE SOUTH of the dam an outcropping of rock, perhaps twenty feet high, jutted out from the east side of the canyon like a small promontory. The floor of the canyon curved to the west, around the barrier, then turned east, along the south side of the outcropping. Directly ahead, against the canyon wall, was Powerhouse Number 2. At the powerhouse, the canyon returned to its southbound flow through San Francisquito Canyon.

It took but a fraction of a minute for the wall of water, a hundred twenty feet high, to slam into the outcropping – some of the raging torrent rushing around it, but most of the flood passed over the twenty-foot-high promontory as if it were a mole hill.

POWER HOUSE NUMBER TWO was a solid structure that stood sixty-five feet high but was tiny compared to the massive torrent that slammed into it, crushing the building like a large foot stepping on an empty match box. More than sixty employees and their families who were inside the building died instantly.

A short distance southwest of the power house, in the bed of the canyon, were a collection of cottages where employees assigned to the power house lived. Lyman Curtis was off duty and was at home with his wife, Lillian, and their three children – two small girls and their two-year-old baby brother. Upon hearing the sound of the flood crashing into the power house, Lyman yelled for his wife to grab the baby and rush to the east bank of the canyon and make her way to the top. He would grab the girls and follow.

It was a struggle, but Lillian, with the baby cradled in one arm, managed to make it to the top, where she sat heavily on the ground, panting. After quickly checking to make sure her son was ok, she stared downhill, in the direction from which Lyman and the girls would be coming. It was dark and she could not see beyond a few feet. Had she been able to look farther, she would have discovered that their house was no longer there. It was being washed down the canyon. She would never again see her husband and two daughters in this life.

A hundred yards down the canyon from the Curtis home, Ray Rising, another power company employee, was awakened inside the tiny house where his wife and child were sound asleep. Rising was awakened by a thunderous sound. He got out of bed and stepped out the front door. It took less than a second for him to realize the danger. He started to run back into the house to awaken his family, but it was too late. The structure began shaking and he was thrown to the ground. As the water was upon him the house was loosened from its foundation and joined in the rush of water that carried it downstream. Ray Rising would later state that he could not explain how the house was taken, yet he remained on the ground. As soon as the initial surge of the enormous wall of water passed it was followed by a rapid flow from the dam. A moment later the rooftop of a small house, or shed, passed close to where Rising had fallen. He made his way to his feet and waded toward the structure then grabbed onto the roof, for the lower portion was submerged. The structure moved downstream at an angle toward the east bank. When it reached the far side of the gigantic rush of water, Rising took a chance and jumped onto the bank a brief second before the structure smashed into the side of the canyon and broke apart, the kindling lost in the continuing onrush of the raging torrent. Rising crawled rapidly away from the bank until he felt reasonably safe from the flood. As he sat on the ground it suddenly occurred to him that his wife and child were gone. As the days of search and rescue passed he managed to reconcile himself to the fact that he would never see either of them again.

While Ray Rising was fighting to save himself, the torrent continued to move southwest and through the tiny settlement where many of the power company employees resided. None of the structures, including the schoolhouse, were left standing. By now the number of fatalities was growing rapidly. Of the employees assigned to the power house, and their families, Ray Rising, Lillian Curtis and her two-year-old son, were the only survivors.

Moments later the flood reached the Santa Clara River, moving across to the far banks, where it overflowed, blanketing the flatter land beyond with several feet of water. The greater portion of the billions of gallons, however, turned west by southwest, following the path of the river, where gravity would take it to the Pacific ocean, more than fifty miles from where it entered the river. At the site of the dam the altitude was over two thousand feet above sea level. By the time the flooding waters entered the Santa Clara River the elevation had dropped to one thousand feet in its race to the ocean.

Ten minutes later, moving west/northwest from where the torrent joined the river, the massive flow crashed into the bridge along the Ridge Route, a major artery connecting Los Angeles with the San Joaquin Valley, smashing the structure into splinters, and leaving a deadly trap for any vehicles north or southbound on the highway. It was a dark night, and the headlight beams on cars were not strong enough to penetrate the darkness for any distance. Before the cars' occupants realized the danger, the vehicles were tumbling into the turbulent cauldron below.

AN HOUR EARLIER forty-eight-year-old Christopher Boswell sat at a table outside his tent at the Edison Camp near the banks of the Santa Clara River. Across the table sat a younger man. On the table was a chess board. The younger man reluctantly moved his rook forward three spaces. Boswell smiled and moved his queen diagonally and captured the rook, then announced, "Checkmate."

"That's the fourth game in a row that you beat me." Scratching his head, he asked, "Who taught you this game anyway?"

"Believe it or not," Chris began with a deep western drawl, "I learned to play the game from a former gunfighter back in Texas."

"No kidding!" the younger man exclaimed. "What was his name?"

"Clay Barnhill. At one time he was known as Whispering Clay Barnhill."

"Never heard of him."

"I'm not surprised," Boswell replied. "From what he told me, the reputation was short-lived. Besides, it happened back in the 1860s, long before I was born."

"How'd you happen to meet him?"

"He was an acquaintance of my father."

"Was your father a gunfighter?"

"No. My father was a preacher."

"How in the world did a gunfighter and a preacher ever get together?"

Boswell grinned. "It's a long story. Maybe I'll tell it to you some day." He paused long enough to stretch and yawn. "But it's late, and we have to get up early tomorrow. We have to be sure the Edison bigwigs know their work camp is giving them a full day's work. These electric lines aren't gonna string themselves."

As the two men made their way to their respective tents, Chris Boswell continued to reflect on his childhood back in McAllister, Texas. He was less than a year old when his father accepted an offer to preach in the little town. Years later Chris' older brother, Nathan, would follow in their father's footsteps and become a minister, but Chris had a touch of wanderlust in his veins. As soon as he became old enough he left home, and a few years later he found himself in Los Angeles. During his first few years in the City of Angels, he was satisfied with doing odd jobs – just enough to keep him supplied with the bare essentials. Then he met Charlotte and fell in love. This prompted him to go in search of a better paying job, and eventually went to work for the Edison Company, a fairly new business that would, in time, provide electric power to much of the population in Los Angeles County.

And now, here he was camped out north of San Fernando, a stone's throw from the Ventura County line. He was not alone, for there were one hundred forty workers in the camp. They had been sent there to string electric lines from Saugus to Saticoy, a distance of forty miles. He liked his job, but he was married with three teenage children – two boys and a girl – and he would much rather spend his nights at home, but commuting was just not practical. It was a job that would take several days, and setting up camp was more convenient than driving from home to the work site every day. For Chris it would be more than an hour's drive each way.

"Oh, well," he reminded himself, "the pay is good."

After closing and securing the tent flaps he lay atop his bedroll that was spread over a wooden floor to which the tent was attached. Not all of the tents were set up over a wooden floor. Chris considered himself one of the lucky ones. Before the night was over he would realize just how lucky he was.

AFTER DESTROYING THE bridge on the Ridge Route, the flood followed a turn with the river in a west by northwest direction toward Castaic. A short distance later the river's course returned to its westward flow, but not before sending a huge wave toward the junction.

The tourist cabins at Castaic Junction had no customers that night. The proprietor's nineteen-year-old son, George McIntyre, was standing outside next to his father, owner of the motor court. They were curious about the strange noise coming from the east. Staring off in that direction, neither father nor son could make out what it was. The seven tourist cabins were all but deserted. He was momentarily distracted when an occasional car rolled past the motor court as it made its way south on the Ridge Route, heading toward Los Angeles, unaware that the bridge had washed out moments earlier. The moon was in its final quarter and was barely visible due to the dark clouds that covered the region. Visibility was extremely poor.

The strange sound grew louder. Flashes of light could be seen off to the southeast, behind the cabins.

"Whatever is going on over there," the elder McIntyre observed. "It's wreaking havoc with the power lines."

Suddenly the ground under them began to shake. Father and son both guessed that it must be an earthquake – except for that eerie roar. That was not the sound that accompanied an earthquake.

George glanced at the tourist cabins and was shocked to see the end cabin moving! It seemed to swirl in a circle and was moving toward them! Suddenly they both felt a rush of water as it swirled around them. The water rose rapidly as it moved up their bodies. The reality suddenly hit them – the St. Francis Dam had busted!

George had to fight the urge to panic, but his father grabbed him as the flow of water began to carry them away. The rush of water was now more than seven feet deep and carrying them both in a northerly direction.

In the midst of this terror, George suddenly thought of his little brother, Billy, who was probably trying to crawl through the window of the room where he had been sleeping. But there was nothing he could do. The flood waters completely controlled both George and his father. Furthermore, the struggle for self-survival was dominant among George's fears.

Still tightly clinging to one another, father and son were carried by the strong current northward toward the town of Castaic. Directly ahead of them was a utility pole. George and his father saw it at the same time. They both grabbed for it as they were about to pass, then clung to it as the raging water pushed against them. Mr. McIntyre, still clinging to his son, urged him to work his way around to the lee side of the pole, while he situated himself on the other side, where the force of the water worked at tearing him away from his son.

A few minutes later Mister McIntyre screamed out in pain. "Oh, my God! I'm hurt!" A moment later he said, "Goodbye, son!" Then he was gone, lost in the churning water.

George was now alone in the swirling nightmare that was trying to pull him to his death. In spite of the terror that gripped him, George managed to keep a level head. He thought that, if he could swim to the north, he might be able to survive, as long as he stayed away from the main channel of the Santa Clara River, which was off to the west.

Then, just as George was thinking he might be moving away from the dangerous part of the churning nightmare, a startling thought occurred to him. He was heading toward the deep wash coming from Castaic Canyon. There was nothing he could do to change direction. Moments later he was being washed down a steep embankment, tumbling head over heels. The water he swallowed was thick with mud. He rolled and was tossed against the embankment as the water continued to pull him down. There was the sense of drowning as he struggled to vomit out the muddy water that was trying to strangle him.

George was rapidly reaching the point of giving up and letting the flood water have its way with him. Then, suddenly, he glimpsed a nearby cottonwood tree that was growing out of the embankment. Reaching out, he grabbed hold of a small branch and managed to hold on with a tight grip. Looking up, he saw a branch that was larger than the one to which he was clinging. With an effort, he pulled himself up to it. For the first time since this nightmare began, George McIntyre felt that he might survive the ordeal. Forcing himself to think of something else, he began examining himself for injuries. In doing so, he was shocked when he learned that he was stark naked. Every stitch of his clothing had been torn from him – including his socks and underwear.

Then, from out of the blue, another thought came to him – was it only yesterday that he was helping his dad work on the T-Model when a plane flew overhead? He had waved to the pilot and the pilot had waved back. It seemed it was ages ago, yet it was only yesterday! His dad and little brother were still alive. If only he could have known then what he knew now. Things would have turned out much differently.

Shortly after daybreak George would be rescued from the limb of the tree on which he had been clinging for the past eight hours. The rescue workers had to plead with him to come down. Eventually he did so and was treated at the closest first aid station. George would eventually recover from the trauma of the previous evening, but it would take time.

17

IT WAS SHORTLY after one a.m. when Los Angeles County Deputy Sheriff Paul Nester turned the 1926 Model T Ford sedan into the driveway of the Temple City Sheriff's Station. As he entered the small, empty building the phone rang. Nester, being nearest to the phone, answered.

"Temple Station, this is Deputy Nester."

"Paul, what a lucky break you answered the phone!" Nester immediately recognized the voice of his former sergeant at Newhall Station.

Six months earlier Nester had transferred from Newhall to Temple station, a few miles southeast of Pasadena.

"What's up sarge?"

"Plenty! The St. Francis Dam has broken and sent a huge wall of water over the entire area! We need all the help we can get! I'm calling for help from every station!" After a pause, he added, "It's a lucky break you answered the phone, Paul, since you're well acquainted with the area up here."

"How many men do you need?"

"As many as the station can afford. But I want you to be among them!"

After hanging up the phone, Nester called the captain and explained the situation to him. The captain authorized four men to respond, and soon, with Nester behind the wheel, he and three companions were proceeding north through the San Fernando Valley enroute to Newhall.

AT HIS HOME in Santa Monica, Undersheriff Eugene Biscailuz retired early in the evening. He needed the rest, for the following morning he was to deliver a prisoner three hundred miles north to San Quentin Prison. At midnight, however, he received a phone call that changed those plans. The person on the other end was calling from the Newhall Sheriff's Station.

"Looks like all hell has broken loose here, sir!" the distraught voice said. "The St. Francis Dam has gone out! We need you here as soon as possible!"

"Minutes later the undersheriff was fully dressed. He quickly called two friends, who were also executives with the Sheriff's Office. After quickly explaining the emergency to his wife, Biscailuz was out the door and driving to Venice to pick up his companions.

An hour later the car pulled up in front of the Newhall Station. When they entered Gene was mildly surprised to find the station empty, except for a lone sergeant manning the phones.

DEPUTY PAUL NESTER pulled the Model T sedan to the front of the Newhall Station and parked adjacent to a car that he would soon learn was that of the undersheriff. As he and his three companions stepped inside he was greeted by the sergeant. Before the deputies had a chance to find a chair and sit down, the sergeant rushed up to them.

"Paul! I'm glad you're here! Since you are familiar with the country around here, I need you to make your way north, through the back roads, until you figure you are north of Castaic, then make your way west, to the Ridge Route, then drive south on the highway."

"Why the long way around?' Nester asked.

"Because the bridge is out," he paused and tried to hide an emotional catch in his voice. "The bridge is out, and we need men to stop traffic on each side." The sergeant took a deep breath and added, "Several cars have already gone over into the water. Some of them have been washed downstream." The sergeant paused long enough to take another breath, then said, "I already have a deputy on the south side of the bridge."

"We're on our way!" Nester announced.

"Not 'we.' You're gonna have to make this trip alone. I need your companions here. This whole area is a disaster."

Minutes later Deputy Paul Nester was heading north by east along a country road that would allow him to circumvent the disaster inside San Francisquito Canyon.

THE BETTER PART OF an hour passed by the time the deputy turned his patrol car onto the southbound highway known as the Ridge Route, five miles north of Castaic Junction. Except for the modest beam of the vehicle's headlights, it was pitch dark all around him. The deputy drove cautiously as the car moved along the road at forty miles per hour. Moments later Nester was startled when the wheels of the vehicle suddenly splashed in a shallow body of water. Though it was no more than a few inches deep, the presence of the water caused an eerie feeling to come over him. He could see Castaic off to the west. A moment later he noticed, a hundred yards ahead, what appeared to be a large trailer truck parked diagonally across the road. Slowing his speed to twenty miles per hour, he approached the truck cautiously, then came to a stop ten feet from the big rig. On the right side of the road a man held a lantern and waved it from side to side.

Retrieving a flashlight from a satchel on the right front seat Deputy Nester stepped out of the car. Only then did he remember to retrieve his badge from his pocket and pin it to the left lapel of his jacket. Like so many other members of the Sheriff's Department, he wondered when the County would wise up and provide uniforms that would readily identify the deputies. Taking a deep breath, he proceeded toward the man with the lantern.

"You can't park there, buddy," The man declared as he momentarily stopped waving the light. He was a large, middle-aged man with a round face and graying hair that was receding on the sides. "The bridge is out, and you're gonna have to turn around and find another way to get to L.A."

As Nester moved closer to the man, he moved his left hand up and, with his thumb, pushed the lapel of his jacket forward to emphasize the badge that hung on it.

"I'm Deputy Nester, with the sheriff's office. I was sent up here to assist you in any way I can. There's another deputy on the far side of the washout."

An expression of genuine relief swept over the trucker. Extending his hand, he said, "Boy, am I glad to see you! My name's Don." He could not hide the emotion in his voice.

Shaking his hand, Nester said, "Call me Paul. Can you fill me in on the situation here?"

"I can only tell you what I've seen and done," Don replied. After a brief hesitation, he began, "I was driving south from Bakersfield when I came upon a car parked sideways across the highway. I immediately hit the brakes and stopped just before I hit the car. When I climbed down out of my rig I was ready for a fight. But the man ran up to me, shaking and scared half to death. He explained that the bridge over the river was out.

"I've been driving this route for over two years, and I knew he was talking about the Santa Clara. He went on to say that some vehicles had already gone into the water, including a bus. No telling how many passengers it was carrying." Don paused briefly while he collected himself. "The man said he had been trying to stop cars by flagging them down. Some heeded his warning, while others drove on past."

Don shook his head. "That's when I decided to park my rig across both lanes of the highway. The cars would have to stop … or plow into me." The trucker paused before adding, "I never got the man's name. It's sad because I think I owe him my life. My rig could very well have been one of those vehicles in the river now."

"What happened to the man?" Nester asked.

"Shortly after I arrived, he got in his car, turned it around and headed north." Don reflected on what he had just said, then added, "Can't say as I blame him one bit."

"Well, Don," Nester said, "What do you say you show me the damage to the bridge."

The trucker shook his head. "Can't show you the bridge. The whole thing has been swept down river." He hesitated briefly, "But I'll show you where it used to be."

As the two men sloshed through ten inches of water Don warned, "We have to move slowly. The water we're walking through is actually the water level of the river, and I sure don't want to step off into it. That river must be forty feet deep."

As they moved slowly toward the river Don said, "I've driven trucks all over the country these past twenty years, and I've had occasion to see flash floods. But I swear I've never seen anything like this."

"This wasn't a flash flood," the deputy replied. "You ever hear of the St. Francis Dam?"

"Can't say that I have."

"I'm not surprised. It was only two years old. Anyway, it was a huge dam. Held several billion gallons of water, or so I'm told. Anyway, the dam burst a few hours ago and sent most of its water down into the river." Nester paused before adding, "I suppose most of the water has passed here already. It'll continue moving west along the river all the way to the Pacific Ocean – about forty-five or fifty miles from here."

Don suddenly held out his arm to stop the deputy from moving farther. "This is as far as I dare go. We're pretty close to the river bank."

Paul Nester stared southward but saw nothing but glistening water as far as the darkness permitted. He had worked in this area of the county for a few years and was quite familiar with the bridge. It had spanned the peaceful-flowing Santa Clara River – a river that was seldom more than a few feet deep but with a depth now of forty feet, even though the raging torrent from the dam had already passed this point. The water level would eventually dissipate, but not until the initial wall of water made its way to the ocean.

At Don's urging, Paul stared down into the depths of the river. There were dim lights scattered along the bottom. The trucker pointed out that those were the headlights of cars that had been driven into the water. Inside each car were the driver and passengers, having been trapped inside and were now dead.

The trucker shook his head sadly. "Those cars went over before I got here. I'm thankful that none went over after I parked my truck across the highway." He breathed a deep sigh, then added, "There's not much traffic at this time of night, but I did manage to turn a few cars back." He looked in Paul's direction and frowned. "I just wish I had been here to stop the bus that went over. You can't see it down there now. It was washed down river earlier – when the current was much stronger."

As they made their way back to the truck Don asked. "How long do we have to be here?"

Paul thought for a moment, then replied, "Well, I suppose you can leave any time you want. You've already done more than your share." The deputy shook his head slowly. "But I'd sure hate to see you go before daylight. Your rig is the main obstacle preventing traffic from going into the river. At sunrise there will be repair crews showing up. They'll bring official barricades to block traffic until a bridge can be erected."

The trucker was silent for a moment before offering a smile. "Don't worry, Deputy. I'll stick around as long as you need me."

18

THE FLOOD WATERS continued down river toward the Edison Camp. The torrent overflowed the banks of the river by thirty feet and spread over the landscape, north and south of the river, for the better part of a mile in each direction. The elevation was now about eight hundred feet, and gravity continued to pull the massive flood waters ever closer to the Pacific Ocean.

The Edison Camp, on the border of the Los Angeles and Ventura county line, was only minutes away from Castaic. One hundred forty men slept in their tents, unaware of the danger that was upon them.

Ed Locke was the Edison Company security officer assigned to keep watch as the men slept in their tents. He took his job seriously. But like everyone in the area, he was completely unaware of the approach of the watery behemoth that was only minutes away from the camp. He could hear a sound from the east but concluded that a heavy wind storm was heading their way. Suddenly bright lights appeared briefly off to the east as transmission lines tumbled to the waters below.

The massive body of flood waters, spreading over the land, continued to move west, parallel with the flow of the river, on its journey to the ocean. On this course, the unstoppable flood moved ever closer to the Edison camp. Ed Locke never had a chance to sound the alarm, for he was one of the very first to be hit by the massive flood.

The thirty-foot wall of water struck the camp with a swift and powerful force. The campers who had taken the time to button up their tents would be among the survivors. The majority of workers, sadly, had left their tent flaps open. The flood waters entered the tents and ripped them off the ground, the occupants unable to extract themselves from within. Having no idea what had hit them, they were tossed around then thrown against boulders and trees that were large enough to survive the onrush of water.

The occupants perished without knowing what had struck them. The flood continued west, leaving the campground a mass of carnage. Among the wreckage of cars, trucks, power poles and cable, as well as heavy equipment, were the lifeless bodies of eighty-four workers. Later, inside the tents of the dead, claw marks could easily be seen where the men had desperately tried to claw their way out of the canvas death traps.

Nearby, a massive whirlpool developed when the westbound flood met a pool of still water. One of the workers who had escaped the confines of his tent less than a minute earlier, was caught inside the whirlpool and struggled to keep his head above water as he was spun around several times. Fortunately, the centrifugal force was powerful enough to throw him clear of the whirlpool. He was one of the survivors.

At dawn workers found the body of Ed Locke, the security officer. He had been wearing a top coat. When the water hit, the arms of the top coat had become pinned to his body, which made swimming impossible.

Another of the workers became so traumatized that he actually went temporarily insane. Breaking away from his tent, he ran, nude, into the hills that rose up north of the camp.

Rescuers found him two days later. The trauma had not left him, and he refused help from anyone. Eventually, however, the rescuers convinced him to accompany them to a relief station. Within a few months he would be back at work for the Edison Company.

Christopher Boswell, having buttoned up his tent, was one of the lucky ones. As he worked to free himself from the canvas enclosure, his head poking through a tear in the tent, he was shocked and dismayed at the carnage that lay before him. Others, who had managed to free themselves from their tents, were walking about aimlessly, numbed to the wreckage around them.

After extracting himself from the tent, Chris set about searching for the young man with whom he had been playing chess the night before. They had become friends during the past few days and tended to stick together on the job. He spent most of the day in search of the young worker, but never found him. Days later the young man's body would be recovered several miles downstream.

FROM THE DISASTER at the Edison Camp the massive surge of water proceeded west, across the Ventura County line, toward the small communities of Camulos, Piru and Fillmore. The ground on either side of the Santa Clara River was fairly flat, though there were hills scattered throughout the valley that rose to a height that promised safety from the flood waters now rising twenty feet above the banks of the river. This was an area where vast orchards of walnut trees, as well as avocado and orange trees, covered the landscape. The orchards were grown commercially by wealthy land owners who did not reside in the immediate vicinity. The fruit was picked by Mexican families who lived in hovels that were scattered among the vast orchards.

The flood water spread over the orchards, destroying numerous trees, as well as the homes of many of the migrants. While the impact of the spreading water was not as great as was the powerful surge that proceeded along the river, its damage to the trees was significant. The water also brought with it a terrible stench – a mixture of death, rot and foul water not unlike that of a cesspool. Though there were many casualties, most of the migrants managed to evacuate to higher ground and survive the deluge.

It was in this general area, a few miles east of Santa Paula, that the bodies of George McIntyre's father and young brother would be found – almost thirty miles from the motor court near Castaic.

19

IN THE TOWN of Santa Paula, ten miles west of Fillmore, Thornton Edwards was awakened by the incessant ringing of the phone. Lifting the receiver, he answered with a sleepy 'hello?'

"Officer Edwards?" the woman's voice on the other end asked.

Thornton smiled into the phone. "Good morning Miss Gipe. To what do I owe the pleasure of your sweet voice?"

"Never mind that!" the phone operator replied in an official tone. "I'm calling to inform you of a flood along the river that is heading toward Santa Paula!"

"A flood? From where?"

"From the St. Francis Dam, east of the Ridge Route!"

"Never heard of it."

"Neither had I until a minute ago! Be that as it may, there's a huge wall of water heading this way along the river. It's overflowing the river bank by several feet!"

"Do we have any idea how much time we have?"

"They're guessing about an hour and fifteen minutes."

All attempts at levity vanished as the seriousness of the situation struck Edwards. "Thanks, Miss Gipe! I'll get dressed and alert the town!"

Edwards leaned across the bed and quietly nudged his wife. A light sleeper, Ethel awakened, turned onto her back and smiled at her husband.

"Honey, an emergency has come up. There's a flood heading our way along the river. It's overflowing the banks by several feet."

Ethel stared questioningly at her husband. "A flood?" she asked.

"Where is it coming from?"

"The St. Francis Dam has broken."

"Where is that?"

"I have no idea, but I need to get out and warn as many folks as I can! Meanwhile, you need to wake up Junior, then call the Carrier Auto Court across the street. Have them call the rest of the inhabitants on South 8th Street. Then load Junior into the car and the two of you leave the area." As he spoke, Thornton was up and quickly dressing.

"Where should we go?"

"Just drive up to the hills behind our house. Maybe up to the school house!" He paused briefly and reflected on what he had just said. "This house is too close to the river to take any chances. I may be gone for quite a while, and I need to know that you and the boy are safe."

Ethel arose and slipped into a bath robe. "Let me fix you something to eat before you go."

"Thanks, sweetie, but I don't have time!" He leaned over and kissed her, then departed.

From the garage that sat adjacent to the house he pushed his 1925 Indian motorcycle onto the driveway. With a single depression on the foot pedal the machine roared into action. Thornton loved his motorcycle and made it a point to maintain it in top running order.

Before departing he glanced back toward the house and noticed that the light was on in his son's bedroom. He smiled, assured that his wife was wasting no time.

His first action was to awaken the neighbors near his residence. At first he went door-to-door, but soon decided that it was taking too much valuable time. He then set up a plan whereby he would arouse every third house, instructing the occupant to wake up the neighbors on either side of his residence. He made a point of reminding those awakened by him that this was a life and death situation, for they were all potentially in the path of the flood.

Still sensing that too much time was being wasted by individually awakening the residents, he decided to start using his siren. Riding up and down the street with siren blowing at a high pitch caused lights to come on from numerous houses. Soon residents began moving about in an attempt to find out what all the ruckus was about.

A few minutes later Thornton was relieved to see Stanley Baker, his fellow motorcycle officer, arrive. "Sorry, Thornton, but I was just advised of the situation."

"That was my fault, Stan." Thornton replied. "I should have notified you first. But I sure am glad to see you now! How about turning your siren on." He grinned then added, "Folks seem to be responding to the noise."

With siren blaring, Stan joined Thornton in alerting those residents whose homes were closest to the river. Moments later the sound of the town's auxiliary fire alarm, quickly followed by the whistle from the nearby Union Oil refinery, left virtually no one in town unaware that a serious emergency was occurring. Minutes later several firemen joined in evacuating residents.

20

IT HAD BEEN the luck of the draw that Ventura County Deputy Sheriff Eddie Hearne had been issued a Cadillac as his patrol car. Not only was it comfortable; it was also fast. Cruising east bound along the highway at a speed in excess of seventy-five miles per hour, his siren blaring, he soon found himself in Santa Paula. He slowed his speed as he drove through the town, surprised to see so many people standing around outside their homes in the middle of the night. His blasting siren blended with the sirens and other alarms from various sources of Santa Paula. As he drove along the highway he suddenly saw a motorcycle officer heading in his direction. As the cyclist got closer Eddie recognized the rider as Officer Thornton Edwards. Although the two lawmen did not know one another well, they were friendly acquaintances.

As the car and motorcycle were getting closer, Eddie Hearne rolled down the window and signaled Edwards to stop. When the two officers were side-by-side, facing in opposite directions, Edwards peered into the Cadillac, which was an unlikely vehicle for a peace officer.

"Eddie Hearne!" Edwards grinned. "What brings you this far east?"

Extending his arm out the window and gesturing toward the activity surrounding them, the deputy replied, "From the looks of things around here, I suspect you already know!" This was followed by a grin. Then the grin faded. "Seriously,

Thornton," Hearne added, "I don't really know what's going on. I was just told there was some kind of a flood heading west along the Santa Clara River, and I'm supposed to get people out of the way."

"There's a flood, all right. From what I've been told, the St. Francis Dam has collapsed, and it is sending billions of gallons of water along the route of the Santa Clara River. We've been told to wake up everybody and have them move to higher ground."

"St. Francis Dam? Never heard of it," Hearne replied.

"That was my first reaction," Edwards replied. "But I'm informed from reliable sources that a flood is, indeed, heading this way."

"Then I better get to Fillmore!" Hearne frowned. "If it's still there."

"Take care, Eddie," Edwards offered. "God willing, you'll get there in time."

A few minutes later a second Ventura County Sheriff's squad car, its siren wailing, made its way slowly through the activity in Santa Paula. The two occupants, Deputies Carl Wallace and Ray Ransdell, stopped only long enough to be given the same information that Hearne had received regarding the flood. Seconds later they were heading east, a few minutes behind the Cadillac.

The town of Fillmore was quiet when Eddie Hearne drove along the main street. There were several people wandering about aimlessly. It was the strange faraway noise that had awakened them. Deputy Hearne suddenly realized that the town had not been alerted to the coming danger. It was quite apparent that the phone call warning from Ventura that was to have been made to city officials in Fillmore had not come through.

Deputy Hearne got out of the car and moved quickly to the nearby fire house and began tugging on the rope to the fire alarm bell. The townspeople aimlessly walking about began congregating around the deputy, and only then were they informed of the impending danger. At Deputy Hearne's direction they scattered in different directions on a mission of alerting the rest of the town to get up and quickly move to higher ground.

Shortly afterward Fillmore Police Chief Earl Hume ran up to Deputy Hearne. "I'm the police chief. What the devil is going on?" he asked.

Surprised, the deputy stared at the chief. "You haven't heard?"

"Heard what?" There was both concern and anguish in the police chief's words. "I just happened to wake up when the fire bell began clanging!"

"I'm sorry, Chief," Hearne replied. "The sheriff's office in Ventura has been trying to call you for the past hour or so. I guess the line is down somewhere." The deputy went on to explain the situation that lay before them.

"Thanks, Deputy," the chief replied. "I'll take over the evacuation from here. How about continuing east to get an idea of how much time we have before the flood gets here."

Offering a wry smile, the deputy replied, "Will do, Chief. Those are my orders, anyway; to go as far as I can to get an idea of how much time we have."

Following a brief pause, he added, "There are two other deputies behind me. When they get here, use them as you see fit until I return."

A moment later Eddie Hearne was driving eastbound on the highway. Then, after crossing the Pole Creek Bridge, east of town, he brought the Cadillac to a sudden stop. Directly ahead, within the range of the car's headlight beams, the road suddenly disappeared, swallowed up by a huge body of water. It was moving in a west-by-northwest direction, generally following the route of the Santa Clara River, the banks of which were several feet under the approaching blanket of water. Deputy Hearne suddenly realized that this was the prelude to a much larger mass of water that was not far behind. In the brief seconds it took to turn the car around and retreat back over the Pole Creek Bridge, Hearne could see outbuildings from farms, numerous uprooted citrus trees and other debris floating atop the encroaching water.

Pulling up in front of the fire station he saw the police chief addressing several townspeople. Hearne was also relieved to see the two fellow deputies who had followed him from Ventura. They were standing near the police chief.

After quickly describing to the chief what he had witnessed moments earlier, he proceeded to the fire station where he placed a call to Ventura and advised them of conditions in Fillmore, which was as far as he was able to go. It never occurred to him to question how this phone line was working while the police chief's line was out. It would remain a mystery.

Minutes later Deputy Eddie Hearne, followed by Wallace and Ransdell in their vehicle, stopped at the Pole Creek Bridge. This was as far as they could go. Several townsfolk gathered nearby to see the flood waters moving across from them. They saw that the road was completely destroyed as far as the darkness would allow them to see.

This was the scene at which the deputies were staring when Deputy Wallace exclaimed, "Listen!"

From somewhere out in the dark torrent came a cry for help. Carl Wallace quickly shed his heavy topcoat and shouted, "Get me that rope from the car! I'm going out there!"

Seconds later Deputy Ransdell returned with the rope. Wallace quickly tied one end of it around his waist then handed the other end to his partner. Without hesitation he jumped into the churning water, still wearing his lighter jacket.

"When the rope plays out, follow me and keep the rope taught," Wallace instructed Ransdell.

At chest high, the water was shallow enough for him to wade, though it was rough going. The farther he moved toward the river the stronger the current became, and he was constantly moving tree limbs, pieces of wood structures and other debris away from him. He was fully aware that he was wading through a grove of fruit trees. It was necessary, therefore, to maneuver between still standing trees in a way that provided a clear path for his lifeline to remain untangled. Then, suddenly, he felt the rope tightening around his chest and realized that the line had played out. A moment later the rope slackened, and Wallace was immediately aware that his faithful partner, Ray Ransdell, had gone into the water after him, providing more slack in the rope.

The cries for help were growing louder, and Wallace continued to move forward. Fixing his eyes in the direction from which the cries were coming, he began to focus on his surroundings. A moment later he looked up and saw movement on the lower limb of a lemon tree. Hanging from the limb was a young woman. On a nearby tree, he could make out the figure of another person – a man. The deputy was taken aback by the fact that neither of them were wearing any clothing.

The woman was crying hysterically. "Save my baby! Save my baby!"

It was then that Wallace noticed that the man was holding on to an infant with one hand and grasping a tree limb with the other. The water level, meanwhile, was now up to the deputy's chin.

He waded toward the tree from which the man and baby were clinging. With some effort he removed his jacket. He then reached up and convinced the man to hand the baby to him. The deputy then wrapped the baby in the jacket. Though the jacket was dripping water, Wallace felt that it might offer a modicum of warmth from the cool March morning. Free from the burden of holding the child, the man made his way down the tree and into the water.

The woman, however, was a different matter. She was reluctant to expose her nakedness to the deputy. Wallace turned his back while the woman made her way down the tree and into the murky water. Her modesty was preserved as she waded in the water, struggling at first to keep her nose and mouth above the surface. The closer they came to the shore, however, the shallower the water became. Deputy Wallace shouted for someone to bring a few blankets from the patrol car. Deputy Hearne obliged by wading into the water far enough out to allow the woman to wrap a blanket around herself. The man was also given a blanket. It would suffice long enough to get them to a shelter, where warmer attire would be available. Once on shore a dry blanket was provided for the baby, allowing Wallace to retrieve his jacket.

Half an hour later the young blanket-clad family was comfortably resting in a shelter in Fillmore. Coffee and pastry were served to them and the deputies. The young man expressed his appreciation several times. The woman remained silent, staring at the floor. Recognizing her need for privacy, Deputy Wallace motioned for his two companions to accompany him outside.

"Since both of you are soaking wet, and having no change of clothes with us," Eddie Hearne began, "why don't we head back to Ventura? Chief Hume seems to have everything under control here, and since we've gone as far as we can, I would say we have accomplished our mission."

When Carl Wallace and Ray Ransdell both agreed, Hearne added, "The Cadillac is the only car to have a heater, and the two of you are soaking wet, so why don't you take my car? I'll drive yours back."

"You got wet, too," Ransdell replied.

Deputy Hearne shrugged. "I'm still dry above the waist. The two of you are soaked up to your necks." With a note of finality he added, "I'm the senior deputy here and I'm telling you, take the Cadillac!" He grinned and added, "God willing, we'll all soon be back in Ventura – warm and dry."

21

WHEN THE VENTURA County deputies passed through Santa Paula, Eddie Hearne found Thornton Edwards and advised him of the situation in Fillmore.

"My guess is that you have forty-five minutes, maybe less, to prepare Santa Paula for the flood."

Shortly after Deputy Hearne departed for Ventura, Thornton Edwards suddenly remembered the Willard Bridge that spanned the Santa Clara. The old iron bridge was a hangout for residents east of town – mostly Hispanics. News of the flood would certainly attract them.

The highway paralleled the Santa Clara River. Edwards' motorcycle roared along the highway. Moments later he arrived at the north end of the bridge and was shocked by what he saw. There were at least a hundred men, women and children, waiting for the flood to arrive. They were excited, for the mood was one of gleeful anticipation of an exciting experience. Most of these were migrant farm workers who had little in the way of entertainment, and the bridge offered them a pleasant place to congregate – a place to briefly escape from the hovels they called home, amid the orchards that claimed most of their waking hours.

The migrants were fond of Officer Thornton Edwards. He was quite friendly, and he was always respectful of the migrants, unlike many of the law enforcement officers with whom they had come in contact over the years.

Thornton's complexion was slightly darker than most gringos, in spite of the fact that he was born and reared in New England and had never set foot south of the border. His hair was dark – almost black, as was the prominent mustache he proudly sported. During his brief movie career, he was occasionally called upon to play the part of a Mexican – usually a bandido.

The bridge was not designed to accommodate motor vehicles, but Edwards rode the motorcycle several feet along the span and revved the engine, being sure that he had gotten the attention of at least a few of the occupants.

"Senor Edwards!" one of the men shouted.

Though he strongly resembled the men on the bridge, Thornton Edwards could barely speak the language. His vocabulary was limited to words he might find on a menu in a Mexican restaurant. But when he motioned with his hands for them to come to him, they all complied. As they approached, Officer Edwards recognized one of the men, Paco Ramirez, who spoke broken English.

Motioning for Paco to come forward, Edwards, summoning his few words of Spanish and flourishing his hands to emphasize his words, he managed to communicate the extremely hazardous situation they were in. They had to vacate the bridge immediately. The coming flood waters would almost certainly destroy the bridge, killing everyone on it.

Paco apparently knew more English than he let on, for he quickly translated the officer's words in a manner that got the attention of everyone, and they all scrambled off the bridge and moved quickly to their homes, where they would gather their few belongings and move toward higher ground.

Shifting the motorcycle to neutral, Edwards backed it up several feet until the wheels were back on solid ground. Shifting into low, he sped west, back toward town. Upon arrival he requested that two of the firemen be assigned to stand guard at each end of the bridge to prevent others from gaining access to it.

ON THE EAST side of Santa Paula were a collection of shanty-type structures. These were the homes of some of the numerous migrant workers who picked oranges in the groves that extended to the east, along the route of the Santa Clara River. The huge tract of land was fairly flat and extended a mile to the north as far as the forest reserve, where the elevation rose to a level that was safe from the flood.

The waters that extended beyond the banks of the river flowed into the orchards, where the numerous migrant families were still in bed awaiting the pre-dawn time to awake and start another long and back-breaking day of picking fruit. The rush of water was not as strong as the torrent within the banks of the river, but it was still a tremendous volume of water, and it moved through the orchards with a ferocity that brought down a large number of the orange trees.

Ten-year-old Soledad Luna and her family were occupants of one such shanty. Her father, Magdaleno, and his fellow fruit pickers had to report to work when the work bell sounded at 5:30 a.m. Normally, the time for Soledad to arise and start the day of assisting her mother, Irene, in preparing breakfast for her father and two brothers was much earlier. There was also a baby sister, eighteen-month-old Hortense. Soledad's maternal grandparents also lived in the tiny house.

On this particular Tuesday morning Soledad was awakened earlier than normal by the sounds of sirens, and a loud, shrieking whistle from the nearby oil refinery. The sound of a motorcycle could be heard as Officer Stanley Baker rode through the cluster of shanties warning residents of the coming flood.

Magdaleno ran next door to make sure his brother, Sisto, and his family were awake and preparing to evacuate. Sisto advised Magdaleno that he overheard the motorcycle officer telling a neighbor that a flood was heading this way and we all had to get out and try to make it to higher ground. Sisto frowned, then added, "Where do we go? The officer said the flood was only minutes away!"

Magdaleno pointed to the stake bed truck parked in front of Sisto's residence. "Why don't we take your truck? We can load our families into the back of it." Magdaleno frowned. "I know it will be crowded, but what else can we do?"

"Let's go!" Sisto exclaimed, then began coaxing his family members into the bed of the truck.

Magdaleno proceeded to the left side of the truck and climbed into the driver's seat as Sisto helped his family members into the bed of the vehicle. His wife, Ynez, entered the truck cab from the passenger side, holding her youngest child in her lap.

Soledad and her siblings followed their mother into the house where Irene placed the smaller children on top of the bed. When Soledad saw her mother get onto the bed, she followed suit. No sooner were the mother and four children atop the box spring mattress than a wave of water crashed into the house, toppling the tiny structure like a large hand sweeping over a house of cards. Miraculously, the bed remained upright and floated free of the wreckage.

At the same time the flood waters struck the house it also slammed into the side of the truck like a battering ram, turning the vehicle on its right side. Soledad stole a glimpse at the overturned truck, but things were moving so fast she could not focus on the disaster, for she was preoccupied with trying to hold onto the mattress and keep the younger children in the center of the makeshift boat. A moment later they were being carried through the orchard, completely at the mercy of the water raging about them.

Soledad had long, dark brown hair that she wore twisted around a ponytail atop her head. This, along with an air of maturity, suggested an elegance of one much older than ten.

The unyielding current, carrying the makeshift life raft ever westward, had traveled less than a quarter of a mile when disaster struck. Among the numerous fruit trees that had withstood the onrush of water, the mattress floated near one that had a low-hanging branch extending from its trunk. Several smaller branches grew out from the limb. As the mattress floated under the limb, some of the smaller branches made their way into the thick mass of hair atop Soledad's head. As the mattress moved forward Soledad was held in place by the strong limb. While the mattress continued on its westward course, the strong branches forced Soledad toward the rear of the tiny vessel. Seconds later she was dangling from the tree limb, her feet hanging helplessly in the water. Her mother and siblings watched in horror as they became separated from their precious Soledad. Rescue was out of the question as the turbulent waters carried them westward toward who knew where. The rough water beat relentlessly against Soledad's small body as she hung in fear beneath the tree limb, her long, beautiful hair entangled in the branches.

AS HE RODE along the main part of town Officer Thornton Edwards was glad to see activity among the residents. It was still quite dark and the presence of so many people was evidence that they had gotten the word and were in the process of evacuating to higher ground northeast of town.

Another thought then occurred to him. There were three dairy farms a mile or so outside of town. While they were west of the highway, the river made a slight turn to the northwest. This put the dairies on the same side of the river as Santa Paula. Had they been on the west side, Edwards would have had no way of getting across the river to warn the occupants, for there were no bridges in the area.

When he pulled into the driveway of the first dairy he caught a glimpse of the farmer near the barn, holding a lantern. He could also hear the lowing of several cows, which was unusual for this time of morning. Milking was still an hour away. It was apparent that the animals were sensing impending danger.

Stopping near the barn, Edwards shut off the engine as the dairyman approached him. The officer had seen the man around town but did not know his name.

"What can I do for you, officer?" the man asked.

"I just came to warn you about a flood that's heading this way along the river. From what we hear it's pretty bad – overflowing the river bank by several feet."

"Well, we're far enough from the river to not be concerned."

Breathing an audible sigh, Edwards replied, a touch of impatience in his voice. "You hear those cows mooing? They're trying to tell you something."

"Like what?" the man replied doubtfully.

"They're warning you of the danger. Now, I can't say if the water will hit you or not, but I'm strongly suggesting to you that you turn them loose into pasture. If they feel the need, they'll drift back enough to be free of any flooding."

The expression on the farmer's face turned from skepticism to genuine concern. "How much time do I have?"

"None! So, you better get busy turning them out to pasture."

As the farmer ran into the barn, Officer Edwards turned his motorcycle toward the road. There were two other dairies that needed to be warned. After this chore was done, he turned back toward town.

On the western edge of town there was a curve in the road known as Steckles Turn. Edwards rounded the curve then proceeded east along Harvard Boulevard. Just as he entered the main road into the business district he was met by the first wave of water, between four and six feet high, that preceded the main body. The impact knocked him off the motorcycle, which slid under the flow of water. Fortunately, the initial wave passed, and the water level dropped to less than a foot deep. The main body of water was not far behind. West of him the flood, which still overflowed the river banks, continued west along the route of the river.

Edwards managed to stand then, and with an effort, lift the motorcycle upright. Realizing that he should not try to start the machine, for fear that water getting inside the casing of the engine could cause serious damage. It was then that he sniffed his wet clothes and made a face. The smell of the flood water was disgusting. Oh well, he thought, nothing I can do about it now.

Pushing the motorcycle through the water, he managed to make it back to Steckel's Turn just as a man in a Model T Ford was approaching from the west. Officer Edwards waved toward the car and the driver stopped.

"Can I hitch a ride as far as Forbe's Garage? I can sit on the cycle and hold on to the door handle." The driver agreed and soon they were off.

The garage was a few blocks east of town and was clear of danger from the flood. Like the other residents of Santa Paula, though it was still dark, Forbes was awake and in his garage when Edwards arrived. While the motorcycle was being repaired, Edwards waited until the work was done. This included draining the engine of all its fluid, and the parts sufficiently dried before replacing the engine's components with fresh oil and other fluids.

About the time Edwards was alerting the dairies, the main body of water reached Willard Bridge, and the impact was devastating. The two firemen guarding the bridge had departed to safe ground several minutes earlier.

As if it were a toy, the water lifted the iron span from its moorings and pushed it along the water for the better part of a mile before the pieces began to separate. One side of the bridge continued with the flow of water while the other side was pushed over the banks of the river and onto the powerful flow of water along the roadway, where the iron bridge railing tumbled like a small block of wood. A short distance farther, the whole side of the bridge then slammed into a house that was set near the river. The iron battering ram hit with such force that the house was knocked off its foundation before collapsing onto the bridge railing. As if fate had played a hand in the drama, this was the home of Officer Thornton and Ethel Edwards.

Along each side of the residential street were the homes that sat closest to the river. The only thing separating the houses from the river were the yards, the highway and the ground nearest the bank of the river. Most of those closest to the river were destroyed and crushed into kindling. The houses farther from the rush of water, for the most part, remained intact, with some having suffered only reparable damage.

22

THE FIRST GLIMMERS of dawn had arrived when Thornton turned his freshly lubricated motorcycle onto the street where he lived. Then, as he neared his own house his heart sank. Bringing the cycle to a stop a few yards from where one corner of the house had stood a few hours earlier, he sat on the seat and stared with disbelief. The scene before him caused momentary shock. The place that had once been his home was now a mass of rubble. He would later learn that the bridge that collided with his house, destroying it, was the very bridge from which his Mexican friends had evacuated shortly before.

His immediate concern was for his wife and son. Did they make it out in time? Were they safe? The fear and shock caused a sickening feeling inside. Taking in a deep breath and letting it out in a sigh, he dismounted from the bike and moved warily toward the rubble before him.

"Thornton?" a voice shouted from the street thirty yards away.

Thornton turned in the direction of the voice of his neighbor, Carl Wiggins, who lived in a house two blocks east of his own. "Hello, Carl." There was a note of despondence in his voice. "How did you make out in this disaster?"

"Thank the Good Lord we came away unscathed." Carl shook his head sadly and added, "Sorry I can't say the same for you."

"Carl, have you seen Ethel and little Thornton?"

A smile suddenly appeared on Carl's face. "As a matter of fact, I have. That's what I was coming over here to tell you. I saw Ethel and the boy up at the school house where several families have gathered. They are all safe and waiting to be given the all-clear signal. My family is still with them." He sighed briefly then added, "As soon as the flood passed, I drove on down to see how bad the damage was."

A wave of relief swept over Edwards. "Thanks, Carl. That's a big relief to me."

"Is there anything I can do to help?" Carl asked.

Thornton Edwards shrugged. "I don't know what can be done. The house is completely gone."

"Well, we can offer you a place to stay until you find something more permanent," Carl offered.

Thornton had to fight a wave of emotion that came over him. "Thanks, Carl. We may very well have to take you up on that."

AN HOUR LATER Thornton brought his motorcycle to a stop in front of the school. The structure sat atop a hill that offered a view of the town, as well as the river, off to the west. Ethel and Thornton, Jr. stood outside the front entrance to the school. They were in the company of several others who were awaiting word that it was safe to return to their homes.

Thornton, Jr., clutching his favorite play thing, a toy train engine, against his breast, recognized his daddy as soon as the motorcycle came to a stop. "Mama! There's daddy!" he shouted.

When Ethel saw her husband she took her son's hand and rushed to meet him. She put her arms around him and squeezed tightly. Tears were streaming down her face as she gently pulled away and allowed him to kneel down to hug their son.

"I'm ready to go home, sweetheart," she announced, and was surprised to see the distraught look appear on her husband's face as he stood up and faced her.

"What is it?" she prompted.

"It's our house." After a brief hesitation he added, "It's gone. The flood destroyed it."

The expression on Ethel's face was one of both shock and fear. "Destroyed! What will we do?"

"I was just talking to Carl Wiggins. He invited us to stay with them until better accommodations can be found."

"What about all of our stuff? The furniture? Our photos and other personal items?" she asked.

"I don't know, sweetheart. When we get down there we can go through the wreckage and see what items can be salvaged."

"Daddy," Thornton, Jr. asked, "What about my train set?" The youngster's favorite toy was an electric train set he had received two Christmases before. His dad had constructed a large model train table in a room over the garage. Thornton, Jr. loved it so much that the train's locomotive became his constant companion. When he was a few years younger, while most children slept with a stuffed toy, Thornton, Jr. often slept with his locomotive. It was also the only item that accompanied him when he and his mother fled to the school that morning.

WHILE OFFICER EDWARDS was driving his small family back to the wreckage that had been their home, rescue and recovery efforts were already underway in and around Santa Paula. Carcasses of animals of every size and shape were strewn throughout the countryside. The remains of numerous human victims, mostly among the migrant community, were plainly visible as the waters began to slowly recede. Boy scout troops were dispatched to search for these unfortunate victims. They carried poles with flags attached to the ends. Whenever they came upon a deceased victim the scouts would stick a pole in the ground to alert the authorities of the victim's location.

North of where the search began Soledad Luna hung helplessly from the tree limb. As time slowly passed she became almost frozen with fear. This was exacerbated whenever the carcass of a cow or sheep floated past, vaguely illuminated by the moon as its light found an opening in the clouds. Most terrifying was the occasional human corpse that passed under the tree that held her captive.

As she gazed down at her body, which had been robbed of all of its clothing, she cried out in shame. She wanted to ask God to take her life. Though she knew that it was sinful to have such thoughts, the idea of being found in this state was more than she could bear.

This was her state of mind when she heard footsteps of someone slogging through the mud. A moment later a man, who appeared to be about the age of her father, came into view. When he saw Soledad he stopped, taken aback by the sight. As he moved toward her the man removed his overcoat. He was a tall man, and by stretching his arms upward he was able to drape the coat over the back of her shoulders. Soledad reached up and pulled the garment around to the front of her body and buttoned it. A wave of relief came over her as she managed to softly utter a thank you to her rescuer.

"What's your name," he asked softly.

"Soledad Luna," she replied in a barely audible voice.

"Nice to meet you, Soledad. You can call me Mr. Baxter." He smiled, then continued. "I live nearby and was out looking for my dog. He's a big Collie." He gazed up and grinned. "You haven't seen him, have you?"

In spite of her predicament, Soledad could not help but smile. She decided that she liked this man.

"I just live a short distance from here," Mr. Baxter said. "I am going to run home and get a ladder. I'll be back in just a few minutes. Then we'll get you down from there."

In less than half an hour Mr. Baxter returned and climbed up to the branches that had ensnared Soledad. After cutting them away he held onto her underarms and carefully eased her a few feet to the ground. Once on the ground he used a large pocket knife to cut away at the branches still caught in her hair.

As he worked, Mr. Baxter informed her of a rescue shelter that had been set up in town.

"I can't go like this, Mr. Baxter," Soledad replied, a frightened look on her face.

"Well, then, why don't we drop by my house and see what my wife can put together for you?" When Soledad did not respond at first, Mr. Baxter said, "My wife is a small woman." He winced, then added, "Not as small as you, but I think you will feel much more comfortable wearing lady's garments."

An hour later Soledad, attired in a loose-fitting outfit provided by Mrs. Baxter, sat in a chair near a pot-bellied stove in the rescue shelter. As memories of her personal dilemma began to fade, thoughts of her family came into focus.

Did her mother and siblings survive? What about her father and grandparents, and aunt, uncle and cousins? Were they still alive? She would soon have the answers, but for now all she could do was pray.

23

EAST OF CAMULOS was the del Val rancho, a beautiful estate recently purchased by Mr. and Mrs. August Rubel. The house was surrounded by several acres that sat far enough away from the devastating waters that most of their property remained dry – including the house.

Dawn was just breaking when Mrs. Rubel looked out her window and was shocked at what she saw. A man, completely nude, was moving unsteadily toward the house. She immediately called her husband over and he, too, was dumbfounded at the sight.

"Wait here," he said, then went to the bedroom and grabbed a blanket before proceeding to the front door. Opening it, he moved cautiously toward the man. As he neared their visitor Mr. Rubel noticed a look of shock and bewilderment on the man's face.

When he came face-to-face with the stranger, he asked, "What can I do for you?"

The man stared at him through glassy eyes. "The water. So many dead."

"Where?" Rubel inquired.

"At the Edison Camp. All drowned." The man paused and his lips began to quiver. "Help me! Help me!" His whole body was shaking. It was obvious that the man was in shock.

Mr. Rubel draped the blanket around the stranger and escorted him to the house. Inside, he had the man sit down on the living room sofa. Without comment, Mrs. Rubel went to the kitchen and put the coffee pot on the stove. It had been left over from breakfast, and only needed to be reheated.

Several minutes later, after taking a few sips of coffee, the stranger's shivering began to subside. His shaking hands settled, and he was able to finish the hot refreshment.

"Thank you," he said softly.

Mr. Rubel went to the bedroom and returned, holding a pair of work pants and a long-sleeved shirt. "When you are able, you can put these clothes on." He paused and offered a friendly smile. "I think you will feel better."

The man nodded silently then began to rise from the sofa. Mr. Rubel escorted their guest to a back room and assisted him in donning the proffered clothes.

Upon returning to the living room, the man proceeded to describe the nightmare he had experienced at the camp. "I was asleep in my tent, when suddenly it seemed to rise up and started twisting around. I tried to break out of the tent, but it was tied closed. I began to panic, not knowing what in the world was happening. The tent slammed onto a rock – or something hard, then rolled off. The rush of water pushed me again and carried me some distance." The man paused long enough to take a breath and regain his composure. "After a while I was able to make my way out of the tent, but, as soon as I did, a wave picked me up and carried me, through the swirling water – I don't know how far, but eventually it seemed to push me off to the side, where the water was shallower, and not moving very fast. I stood up and moved as fast as I could to dry ground." Offering a weak grin, he added, "Well, it wasn't dry. In fact, the ground was muddy as all get-out, but at least I was out of the running water." He offered an embarrassed grin. "It was at this time I noticed that I wasn't wearing any clothes. The rushing water stripped me naked." He glanced at Mrs. Rubel. "Sorry ma'am."

Offering a sympathetic smile, Mrs. Rubel replied, "Don't apologize. You've been through a terrible experience."

As the day wore on several more refugees from the camp wandered onto the ranch, and their hosts gave each of them the same aid as the first. At one point Mr. Rubel began to wonder if he might run out of pants and shirts for his guests. Each one was given hot coffee and hot food. Soon, they would be back home with their own families, but none of them would ever forget the Christian kindness of Mr. and Mrs. Rubel.

AFTER MOVING PAST Santa Paula, the flood continued its destruction westward. Telephone warnings to Saticoy, Montalvo, Ventura, as well as rural farms and other entities, were delivered all along the river from Santa Paula to the ocean.

The elevation of Saticoy was 157 feet. News of the flood had arrived at that community as early as forty-five minutes after the dam broke, and most of the inhabitants had evacuated to higher ground. Among the inhabitants who ignored the initial warnings were the members of a hobo camp who made their home under the Saticoy Bridge, which spanned the Santa Clara River. After being warned by a nearby rancher, eighteen of the nineteen inhabitants heeded the warning and evacuated. The nineteenth stubbornly refused to leave, insisting there was not enough water in Southern California to allow a man to take an all-over bath, let alone wash away a hobo camp.

The rush of water reached the Saticoy Bridge, where the flood level rose to a level that covered the bridge's floor. The speed of the flood was now one-third what it had been when it began its destructive journey down the Santa Clara River. At this point the flooding behemoth consisted of only fifty per cent water. Twenty-five percent was mud, and the remaining twenty-five per cent consisted of animal carcasses, trees, limbs, trash; as well as cars, trucks, tractors and other machinery. The several houses that had been swallowed up by the deluge were nothing more than splinters of wood. The slower speed and the dissipation of water resulted in the dispensing of much of its debris. The fields along the path of the river were littered with automobiles, wagons, tractors, trees, parts of bridges, as well as the remains of humans and animals that had been ensnared in the rushing flood waters. Recovery would soon become a priority in that part of Ventura County. It was along this route that the body of Chris Boswell's chess friend would be recovered. Nearby, another body was found. It was that of the hobo who had refused to leave his camp under the bridge.

A few miles downstream from Saticoy the Montalvo Bridge crossed the Santa Clara River. Constructed in 1898, it was that section of Highway 101 that spanned the river. The force of the flood had not yet reached this far west, but it was on its way. County patrolman Ken Murphy had been dispatched to guard the north side of the bridge. Another patrolman stood guard on the south side. A few minutes before the flood waters arrived a bus from Pickwick Stage Lines rolled up to within ten feet of Patrolman Murphy. When the officer motioned for the bus to stop, the driver did so, then angrily stepped out of the conveyance and approached the officer.

"I'm sorry, sir," Murphy announced apologetically. "The bridge is unsafe."

The bus driver looked over the span and announced, "It looks fine to me! I'm on my way to Los Angeles, and it's imperative that I get across!"

"I'm sorry, sir. Flood waters are expected to come through here any moment now!"

The officer could see the roll of flood water approaching. Before he could comment, the bus driver offered another protest. He barely began to get the words out, however, when the waters struck the bridge, taking out two hundred feet of the span. The bus driver's jaw dropped, and he was speechless. As he turned and moved slowly toward the bus he became almost ill as he thought of the passengers who might have perished because of his arrogance.

SOLEDAD LUNA'S MOTHER and siblings managed to cling to the mattress as it was carried along the path of the flood's overflow into the farmland of Ventura County. They would finally make landfall somewhere between the towns of Ventura and Oxnard. If the mattress had not run aground, there was a chance it might well have carried its passengers out to sea.

Soledad would soon learn that her immediate family, including her father, had survived the ordeal. Miraculously, her grandparents, as well as her aunt and uncle, also made it through the disaster. Sadly, five of her cousins were lost in the flood's wrath.

BY THE TIME most residents of Los Angeles and Ventura Counties were rising to begin another day the flood waters had reached the Pacific Ocean. It would take time for all the water to dissipate. Over the following days and weeks, the remains of humans and animals would be found along the beaches north and south of the river bed, and as far out to sea as the Channel Islands off the California coast.

TUESDAY
March 13, 1928

5: 20 A.M.

EMMETT HOLLISTER WAS beside himself with anger and frustration. An hour earlier he and his companions had been inside Red Rock Canyon, where the disposal of the explosives went as planned. After burying the dynamite sticks, as well as the fuses, in a deep hole, then filling in the hole, Merle Clinton and Albert Slocumb, at Hollister's direction, had rolled a nearby boulder, eighteen inches in diameter, over the hole. It was a struggle, but they succeeded in setting the huge rock in place.

Satisfied that the incriminating evidence had been safely hidden, the three conspirators then moved to the Model T and climbed inside, Hollister at the wheel. They had proceeded a hundred yards when something appeared at the side of the sandy road, then it suddenly darted into the headlight beams of the car. Instinctively, Hollister jerked the wheel to the right in an attempt to avoid hitting it. As he did so, the right rear wheel rolled atop a large boulder that had a downward slant on one side and a sheer drop off of two feet on the forward side. At the base of the two-foot drop was a second boulder. The car's axel struck that boulder with a loud and frightening impact.

Scrambling out of the car, the three conspirators dropped to their knees to examine the damage. Having no flashlight, one of them struck a match. Defeat swelled within them as they looked upon a bent axel. The right rear wheel and hub sat askew at the side of the car. It was obvious that the vehicle was inoperable.

Several minutes later, having retrieved their personal belongings from the car, the three would-be saboteurs moved despondently along the narrow lane toward the exit of Red Rock Canyon. As they trudged through the sandy ruts of the road a jack rabbit watched from a ledge along the wall of the canyon, unaware of the disaster it had caused by darting in front of the car.

And now, upon reaching the dirt road that, in time, would become Highway 14, they began walking, defeatedly, in the direction of Lone Pine. There was virtually no traffic along the road, and the occupants of those few vehicles that did roll past were not inclined to pick up three strangers who bore a strong resemblance to vagrants.

Four days later, their personal belongings discarded along the roadway, they staggered, half starved, into Lone Pine. Their trek, however, was not quite over, for the three conspirators still had another fifteen miles to walk before reaching their homes in Independence.

VI:
RECOVERY,
RELIEF
AND REGRET

24

IT WAS SHORTLY after daybreak when William Mulholland and Harvey Van Norman arrived at the site of the collapsed dam. When the Chief was first notified by phone of the tragedy, he replied, "God, don't let people be killed!" An hour later, joined by Harvey Van Norman, he would learn the horrible truth.

The driver remained in the car up on the road while the two water company executives carefully made their way down the side of the canyon. The canyon bottom still had a modest flow of water that was moving slowly down stream. The side of the canyon was still wet, but the two men managed to keep their footing. Halfway down Mulholland stopped. He was able to have a clear view of the break, as well as the now empty canyon.

Van Norman followed the gaze of his boss and thought how strange everything looked from yesterday morning, when they had visited the dam and determined that it was safe. There had been some concern on the part of the dam keeper regarding a minor leak, but it was nothing that required any immediate action. Minor leaks were common in dams. To be on the safe side, however, they had thought of lowering the water level over the next several weeks. It just did not seem that urgent at the moment.

Van Norman turned his gaze back to his boss and was saddened by the Old Man's appearance. He was seventy-three years old but looked ten years older. The past several hours had taken a toll on the man who ran the water company. Bringing water to Los Angeles had been his relentless goal since arriving in Los Angeles more than fifty years ago. It had become his life, often putting the needs of his family on hold while he attended to the water needs of the city.

He had become a self-taught hydraulic engineer, and the completion of the aqueduct, the longest of its kind in the world, had earned him great acclaim, and he had been called upon to offer advice throughout the United States regarding the construction of dams. At present, he was serving as an advisor on the Boulder Dam planning committee. It was anticipated that construction would begin within the next few years.

Stealing another glance at his boss, he noted that the Chief was staring downstream, in the direction of the cottage where Tony Harnischfeger had lived with his common law wife and young son. There was no sign of the modest structure. It was as if it never existed. The Harnischfeger family was almost certainly the first victims of the disaster. The expression on his face reflected Van Norman's own state of thought. The Chief was undoubtedly recalling their meeting the day before. What words were exchanged between the Boss and the dam keeper while Van Norman and the driver sat in the car? Whatever they were, he was certain that the Boss desperately wished he could take them back.

At Mulholland's signal, Van Norman turned and carefully retraced his steps to the rim of the canyon, with the Boss close behind. As they moved toward the car Mulholland looked back and stared at the huge piece of wall of the dam that remained standing. Why didn't it collapse with the rest of the structure? It was as if some force allowed the monolith to remain as a reminder of Mulholland's great blunder.

Van Norman, meanwhile, gazed down canyon, where a number of large sections of the dam had been thrown aside by the escaping water. Some of these concrete pieces were the size of car garages, and weighed several tons, yet the enormous surge of water had pushed them downstream like they were empty cigar boxes.

A moment later the two executives sat in the back seat as the chauffeur drove the car on the road toward the canyon's exit. They rode in silence for the first ten minutes, then Van Norman looked directly at his boss and the terrible pain that revealed itself on the older man's face. Though a body count was days, or even weeks, of becoming known, it was obvious that the boss was holding himself completely to blame for the death of each one of them.

"Boss," Van Norman began, "instead of returning to the office, why don't you go home and rest for a few days?"

Mulholland turned and faced his subordinate with an angry frown. "How can I do that? What would I do at home? Do you realize that I am responsible for this catastrophe? Hundreds of people are dead because of me – something I've overlooked! I deserve no more rest than those suffering souls out there!" He waved a hand in the direction the flood waters had traveled hours earlier.

"Boss, at this stage, you don't know what happened. Frankly, I don't think you made any mistakes. Have you considered the possibility of sabotage?" When Mulholland failed to respond, Van Norman continued, "You know the attitude of the folks up in Owens Valley. There are hot heads up there who would think nothing of blowing up the dam!" He stopped long enough to expel a long sigh. "Look at all the acts of sabotage they wreaked on the aqueduct!" He paused again before concluding, "I wouldn't put anything past them."

Unable to persuade the Old Man to go home, the two executives returned to the office.

In April 1928 I attended the opening ceremonies of the new Los Angeles City Hall. Following the ceremonies, I was walking west on Temple Street when I saw none other than my friend, Bill Mulholland. He had just stepped out of the Hall of Justice and was walking east, in my direction. I had not seen him for several months, and I was shocked at his appearance. I'm a few years older than Bill, but I declare, when I got a close look at him, he looked years older than me. Of course, this was about a month after the dam disaster, and the drama was still going strong. The anger toward Bill in some quarters was taking its toll on my friend.

We talked for a few minutes, and at no time did I bring up the disaster, though it was much like trying to ignore the proverbial elephant in the room.

We talked about his kids (who were all grown now and had kids of their own) and how they were getting along. I told him how I was doing. It was friendly, but I could not help but see the perpetual strain on his face. He was taking it very hard, and it hurt me to see him in such bad shape.

We only spoke for a few minutes, then went our separate ways. I ache for that man. He has brought so much to the city, and I pray that he soon finds peace.

25

SITTING FEWER THAN ten miles west of Francisquito Canyon was the town of Newhall. It was, for the most part, outside the reaches of the flood plain of the dam break. It was also the most populous center of business activity in the area. Although many of the town's natives could trace their local lineage back a few centuries, the town was, for the most part, a product of the nineteenth century. There was a western ambiance to which most of the citizens clung.

The town was an unincorporated area of Los Angeles County and was policed by the county sheriff. The local office of the sheriff was located in the heart of the town's business district.

WILLIAM S. HART was at the height of his movie career in 1918, when he leased the 230-acre Horseshoe Ranch in Newhall. Through his own production company, he occasionally used the property to film some of his very popular western features. In 1921 he purchased the property.

Hart continued to make films until 1925. After completing his final movie, *Tumbleweeds*, he retired from the movie business. To his delight, *Tumbleweeds* was a huge success.

Following his retirement Bill moved permanently to the Horseshoe Ranch, where he had a larger, more elegant house built atop a hill above the original ranch house. It was a Spanish Colonial structure with a tiled roof. The large structure contained 7500 square feet of living space. There were six bedrooms and seven bathrooms. In the fall of 1927 Bill and his sister, Mary Ellen, moved into the newly completed house. In a corral at the bottom of the hill, not far from the original ranch house, Bill's famous pinto, Fritz, lived in the luxury that was due him.

BILL HART AND his sister had been living in the newly constructed house less than six months when the St. Francis Dam collapsed. Late that evening Bill was sitting in front of his fireplace, playing *Rosen the Bow* on his ever-present harmonica. The music was suddenly interrupted by what sounded like the firing of a cannon nearby. Seconds later the ground began to shake.

Sitting his harmonica aside, he stood and raced outside. It sounded as if a herd of cattle was running across the ground near the house. From the headlight beams of a passing car the grounds were briefly illuminated, revealing a large flow of water encroaching ever closer to the hill on which the house sat. The headlight beams disappeared, and the grounds were dark again.

Hearing the sound of running footsteps Bill turned to his right and saw his stableman running toward him, a lantern in his hand.

"Mr. Hart!" the stableman called, "I just heard – that dam up in Francisquito Canyon just busted! It's flooding everything!"

Bill Hart and the stableman began lighting bonfires throughout the acreage that made up Horseshoe Ranch. The two of them went in search of survivors who might have been washed onto the property, but soon decided to give it up until daylight.

It was still several hours until daybreak, and though he tried to sleep, his mind kept racing until, at long last, the first rays of daylight made their way into his bedroom.

After briefly advising his sister of what he had observed earlier, he quickly dressed. This time he was more prepared for the elements, having put on high boots and donning a heavy mackinaw coat.

Joined again by the stableman, Hart gazed once more over the acreage that lay before him. In the daylight the water did not seem as high as it had in the middle of the night. Unknown to him at the time, the flood had already reached the ocean shortly before daylight. In a few days the land surrounding the house would be dry.

During the search of the property, the two men uncovered a buried car, from which they recovered four bodies. Hart decided then to turn his garage into a makeshift morgue. Sixteen more bodies were added to the original four, but neither he nor the stableman were able to identify any of them. They had probably been washed onto the property from no telling how far away. Bill Hart was just now beginning to realize that this tragic event was much larger than he first realized.

BY DAWN HELP was showing up at Newhall Station. This brought relief to Undersheriff Biscailuz. He immediately turned the task of rescue and relief over to the Red Cross, as well as companies of the American Legion. Public utilities already had their work cut out for them. Civilian volunteers showed up and Bizcailuz immediately put them to work in various areas. Many of them he deputized to assist the regular deputies patrolling the streets.

One of the men to step forward was dressed in high boots and wearing a mackinaw. His face was unshaven, and he looked exhausted.

"I've got a ranch nearby. I know the area quite well," he said, addressing the undersheriff.

"Get in the car! We can use you!" Biscailuz exclaimed. It was only then that he looked at the man more closely. "Not William S. Hart, are you? The movie actor?"

"That's right."

"Well, hop in, and glad to have you."

SHORTLY AFTER DAYBREAK crews arrived at the sight of the downed bridge on the Ridge Route. Within minutes brightly covered barricades were set up with free-standing road signs extending as far north and south of the river as the nearest junction of a road that would take drivers onto an alternate route to their destinations. In most cases, however, returning to their place of origin was the practical thing to do.

Paul Nester and Don, the truck driver, were officially relieved. Don was a skilled driver and had little trouble turning the rig around. He would head back north, to Bakersfield. At that point he wasn't sure what the owners of the freight he was carrying would ask him to do.

Prior to leaving, Don and Paul shook hands. Paul struggled to find the words to express his appreciation for the trucker sticking around until help arrived. Neither man was much on bidding farewells, and a moment later Paul was watching the rear of the truck as it headed north.

A moment later Deputy Nester was driving on the country road that he had taken to get to this destination. As he drove along he was thinking of Don, and suddenly got the idea of approaching his superiors regarding presenting Don with a plaque, or some such symbol of recognition for his valuable service. He was in the middle of these thoughts when it suddenly occurred to him – he did not know Don's last name, nor did he recall the company that employed him. Breathing a defeated sigh, Deputy Nester struggled to find something else to occupy his thoughts as he made his way back to Newhall Station. Deputy Nester would spend the next ten days taking part in relief efforts, as well as recovery of the bodies of victims.

26

JEFF KIENEST FLEW a course out of Mojave that skirted the south side of the Tehachapi Mountains. With Angela Lundstrum as his passenger in the Curtis Jenny biplane, he had landed at the airfield in Mojave, where he refueled the aircraft, then proceeded on a course that would take them to Newhall. He had been informed by another pilot in Mojave of a ranch outside of Newhall that had an airstrip. They were good folks and were partial to pilots. He was sure they would allow him to land on their field, and for a reasonable price he could probably purchase fuel from them.

Jeff was not familiar with the general area, but he knew that if he stayed on this course he would eventually find the highway known as the Ridge Route. At the highway he would make a turn south and follow the highway as far as the Santa Clara River, which was the flight pattern he had used the day before, only in reverse. At the river he would turn in a southeast direction. Shortly afterward they would pass over Newhall. The ranch with the landing field was a few miles out of town, on the same course.

The highway came upon him unexpectedly. He was looking for a wider roadway, but from a thousand feet above the road the two lanes seemed much like a narrow ribbon stretched along the hills and canyons below. Banking the Jenny to the left, he followed the highway in a generally southern direction. He also noted that there was virtually no traffic on the road.

As Castaic came into view Jeff was suddenly shocked by what he saw. The motor court where he had seen a man working on a car and a younger person waving up at the plane as he passed overhead were completely gone. He grimly realized that this was obviously one of the casualties of the dam break.

He then noticed barricades set up across the highway. At about the same time he noted that the bridge across the Santa Clara River was missing, and he knew that he was looking at yet another result of the catastrophe. He was now beginning to realize the incredible power of this flood. On the south side of the river similar barricades were in place to prevent northbound traffic from driving into the river.

As the aircraft passed over the river he turned the Jenny in a south-southeast direction and headed toward what he hoped was the town of Newhall.

The ground beneath was decidedly rural, with scarcely a structure in sight. Much of it was saturated with water. A few miles farther several small buildings came into view, and he felt confident that it must be the town of Newhall. Following the direction given by the pilot back in Mojave, Jeff continued on the same course.

Five minutes later he saw the airstrip that ran at an angle to a nearby house. Behind the house was a barn. On the side of the air strip from the house a plane, not unlike his own Jenny, was parked. Relief swept over him, though he suddenly realized that, foolishly, he had no plans beyond finding the airstrip.

It was a smooth landing, and Jeff brought the Jenny to a stop before reaching the half-way mark on the runway. To his right the house sat fifty yards away. Before pilot and passenger could loosen their seat belts the door to the house opened and a middle-aged woman stepped outside and moved toward them.

Jeff guessed that she was in her early to mid-forties. Though not fat, she appeared to be slightly overweight. Her dark brown hair was in the early stages of turning gray. Neither Jeff nor Angela made any effort to deplane.

"Sorry for the intrusion," Jeff shouted over the engine noise as the woman was within hearing distance. "I was wondering if you would allow us to park here for a while. We came to help in rescue and recovery at the flood site."

"You can stay a while, but you're going to have to get the plane off the runway. We're expecting a plane in from the city, carrying medical supplies."

"Yes, ma'am," Jeff replied, then began taxiing toward an open field off to his left. He shut the engine off about ten yards from the other biplane he had spotted just before landing.

Jeff and Angela alighted from the plane, then Jeff proceeded to chock the wheels. Following this chore, the two of them moved toward the woman, who had remained on the other side of the runway.

After Jeff and Angela introduced themselves the woman offered a friendly smile.

"My name's Geraldine Summers, but folks call me Geri." She studied the couple briefly before adding, "You mind telling me where you're from?"

"We're from Bishop," Jeff replied. "We heard about the dam break early this morning and thought we might be of some assistance. If they have no use for my plane perhaps Angie and I can be of help someplace else."

"Bishop, eh? Geri began. "That's a long flight for the likes of that ship you're flying."

Jeff smiled. "Is that your plane out there? The one next to mine?"

"Yes, it is. So, you know where from I speak. That relic out there wears me out on a long flight."

Both Jeff and Angela nodded agreement.

"So, how can I be of help?" Geri asked. "Other than babysitting that relic you flew in on?"

"Well, I thought we would locate the command post – that is, if there is one, and see where we can be of help," Jeff said.

"Well, of course there's a command post!" Geri replied, and Jeff couldn't tell if he had offended her. "They're using the Newhall Sheriff's Station. It's in downtown Newhall."

"How far is it from here?"

"It's too far for you to walk," Geri replied, then added, "But if you can wait until the medical supplies arrive , which should be any time now, I'll be driving the supplies to the Sheriff's office in my truck." She smiled and added, "And I'd be pleased to help a nice couple like you."

27

IT WAS MID-AFTERNOON when Jeff and Angela arrived at the Newhall Sheriff's station. The desk sergeant was the only occupant, for everyone else had been dispatched to the numerous areas affected by the disaster.

Jeff explained that he was a pilot, and his plane was parked at the landing field owned by a woman named Geraldine Summers, and he was offering himself and his plane to the sheriff's office to be used however it saw fit.

The sergeant smiled. "I know Geri quite well. I recognized her truck when she dropped you off." Breathing a deep sigh, he added, "At the moment, however, I'm not sure how we could use your plane. We have several in the air right now." Following a brief pause, he added, " But we could use the two of you elsewhere."

"We're available, sergeant. Use us in any way that you see fit."

The sergeant made a face, then asked, "Are you sure about that? It's not a pleasant task, but it's a job that needs to be done."

"Anything will be fine with us," Angela offered.

Taking in a deep breath and blowing it out in a sigh, the sergeant said, "Several temporary morgues have been set up throughout the area, and help is needed at each of them." He frowned. "It's not exactly a glamorous job, but it's vital, and someone has to do it."

"What would we be doing?" Jeff asked as he and Angela exchanged glances."

"As you can imagine, many of these recovered bodies arrive at the morgue in unrecognizable condition. In most cases, their clothing has been ripped off due to the enormous turbulence of the flood waters. Also, they are covered with mud. These bodies have to be cleaned up as much as possible in order to be recognized by neighbors, or, preferably, by the next of kin. I can't say what the professional embalmers will be having you do, but what I've described is probably the least desirable." He stared searchingly at the young couple who stood before him, awaiting their response. "So, what do you say? Are you up to it?"

Jeff Looked at Angela. "I'm going to leave this decision to you. I'll do whatever you say."

"If given the choice, I would much rather be doing something else." Breathing a deep sigh, she added, "But we came here to be of service, and if that is where we are needed, then I say let's do it."

When Jeff nodded his agreement, the sergeant smiled his appreciation, then said, "Good. You two truly are here to help." After quickly studying some papers on his desk, he said, "On the east side of town is a large building that has been set up for demolition but is now being used as a temporary morgue. That is probably where you can be the most help, and it is easy walking distance from here."

After receiving directions from the sergeant, the young couple departed.

WHEN JEFF AND ANGELA entered the large building they caught a whiff of air that was foreign to them, and soon learned that it was the unpleasant scent of Formaldehyde, to preserve the numerous cadavers that lay on quickly constructed slabs atop concrete blocks, makeshift wooden legs and any other item that allowed the deceased flood victim the dignity of not having to lay on the floor. Each victim was covered with a sheet, army blanket or other large cloth that offered a modest covering.

A tall, heavyset man wearing a stained smock approached the couple. "Can I help you folks?" he asked.

"Yes," Jeff replied. "We were sent here from the sheriff's station to offer whatever assistance you might need."

A broad smile appeared as the man said, "That's wonderful. We can sure use you. My name's Oscar Reynolds, owner of Reynolds Mortuary in Sylmar. Right now, I'm functioning as chief mortician – at least at this location. And I must say, we can use all the help we can get."

After Jeff and Angela introduced themselves Reynolds introduced Angela to two other women, both middle-aged, whose job was to prepare the makeshift slabs and blankets in anticipation of the incoming cadavers. Following the embalming process, it was their task to cover the deceased with a blanket and attach the victim's name, if known, around the right big toe.

The mortician then escorted Jeff to the rear of the building and out the back door. A large area, perhaps half the size of the building, surrounded by an eight-foot fence, draped with tarpaulin to cover the view, lay before him. Scattered about the wet ground were several mud-covered bodies of every size and age. The mud covering was so thick on many of them that Jeff was unable to determine their race or gender.

A young man, perhaps in his early thirties, was hosing down a victim lying on a slab. A middle-aged black man, wearing a smock much like Oscar's, though much dirtier, was looking on. When the body was fully cleaned, the black man assisted the younger man in lifting the cadaver onto a stretcher and the two men carried it into the building. As they passed Jeff and the mortician they stopped momentarily.

"Reuben," Oscar said, addressing the black man, "I brought you a new recruit. This is Jeff Kienast, and he wants to help. Jeff, this is Reuben Moss, a fellow mortician." Oscar sighed before adding, "While I would love to have Reuben inside helping with the embalming, I need him out here supervising the cleaning of the new arrivals."

"Nice to meet you, Jeff. I'll be right back to show you around." He and his assistant, a tall thin man who appeared to be in his mid-thirties, who Jeff would learn went by the unlikely moniker of High Pockets, then resumed their task of delivering the stretcher into the building.

The remainder of the day was busy for both Jeff and Angela. Bodies of victims arrived, and Jeff would hose off the mud and other debris that had adhered to the victim, then he and the other volunteer would deliver them into the morgue. On these occasions Jeff and Angela would take the opportunity to meet briefly and check on the other's emotional state. They each assured the other that they were fine.

One of the bodies that arrived was eventually identified as Leona Johnson. Jeff would later learn that she had been the common law wife of Tony Harnischfeger, the dam keeper. Surprisingly, unlike the other victims delivered to the mortuary, this victim was completely clothed. She had been found on the hillside near the foot of the dam, and unlike other victims, she had not been washed away in the flood. It was apparent, however, that she had been crushed by debris from the dam. Jeff washed the mud and debris from her clothing and exposed areas of her skin but could not bring himself to remove her clothes and wash the body more thoroughly. He would leave that chore for the ladies inside the mortuary.

It was late afternoon and the delivery of flood victims slowed. The temporary lull came as a relief to Jeff and his fellow workers. There would be other victims delivered to them, but for the moment the slowdown was welcomed. Jeff stepped into the building and found Angela. Since work had also slowed for the ladies inside, the couple took a break long enough to grab a bite to eat. In an adjoining room was an abundance of food that had been delivered by the women's auxiliary of a local church.

28

IT HAD BEEN a long day for Gene Biscailuz and his companions. Deputy Jim Hardesty was the driver of the undersheriff's car. On the passenger's side was Captain Arthur Jewell. In the back seat sat the undersheriff, and beside him was retired movie actor William S. Hart.

The four of them had joined in the search for victims of the disaster. They had waded in water up to their waists, and in the course of the day had become almost unrecognizable due to the mud that covered them from head to toe.

Captain Jewell, his left arm resting on the back of the seat, turned to address the undersheriff. "Boss, we can't keep working like this."

"What do you mean?" Biscailuz asked.

"We've been working out here since shortly after daybreak, along with literally hundreds of other folks. Some were deputies, some were firemen and other professional folks. But most of them were private citizens. The problem is, we can't tell one from another. I talked to several workers today and didn't even realize I was talking to my own men." He paused briefly, then added, "What I'm getting at is that we need to put our sworn personnel in uniforms so we can easily recognize them."

The undersheriff breathed a long sigh before replying. "There's a lot of horse sense in what you're saying." Following a short pause, he added, "You remind me later, when this operation is over." Changing the subject, he said, "It's getting late. I don't know about you fellows, but I'm beat. Let's head to the station and call it a day." Revealing an ironic grin, he added, "I'm sure there will be more of this tomorrow."

They were nearing the building a few blocks from the sheriff's station that had been designated a mortuary. "I wonder if we could make one more brief stop here." The voice was that of William S. Hart.

"I don't see why not," the undersheriff said, then the driver parked the car in front of the building. Leaning forward, the undersheriff added, "Why don't the two of you relax in the car." Captain Jewell and the driver nodded their appreciation.

The two men entered the building and were immediately approached by Oscar Reynolds. Good afternoon, gentlemen," the mortician greeted. "Can I help you with something?"

Biscailluz, conscious of his and Hart's muddied appearance, said, "I'm Undersheriff Gene Biscailuz and this gentleman is William S. Hart."

A look of genuine surprise appeared on the mortician's face. "Not *the* William S. Hart, the movie actor?"

"The one and the same," Hart replied with a grin.

"I've heard that you live up this way, but I never thought I'd meet you," Oscar replied, then added more somberly, "Especially under these circumstances." Surveying the two men covered in mud he then said, "How can I be of service?"

"Earlier today I was talking with one of the rescuers, and he informed me of a little boy who had been killed in the flood, and they have yet to find the child's family. Sadly, they are of the opinion that the child's entire family was also killed and washed away in the torrent.

"My request is this: if no one shows up to claim the child, I would like to claim him. I will assume responsibility for funeral arrangements and burial expenses."

Oscar assumed a somber expression. "Mister Hart, I can only say that you are every bit the hero you portray in your movies." A sad smile appeared, and he added, "Will you follow me, please?"

Angela and Jeff were emerging from the lunch room when Oscar and his guest approached. "Angela, would you be so kind as to take Mr. Hart to the cot of the little boy that arrived earlier today?"

"Yes sir," she replied, as she stared questioningly at Mr. Hart. There was something vaguely familiar about the man whose clothes were filthy and disheveled, and his face caked with mud.

Jeff, who welcomed the change in the routine of this gruesome day, followed Angela and the man in mud to a cot midway down the row of blanket-covered bodies.

"I believe this is the one to which Mr. Reynolds was referring," Angela announced somberly. She moved to the far end of the slab and pulled the sheet from the child's head. He was a beautiful lad of six, with smooth skin and sandy colored hair. The horror through which he suffered could not remove the innocent expression on his face.

Angela glanced at their guest, and he nodded , indicating that the shroud could be replaced over the child's head.

As they turned to walk away Oscar approached and asked, "Is this the child you were looking for?"

"I'm quite sure it is," Hart replied. He shook his head somberly and added, "I hate to think there are two such children lying dead, without the benefit of loved ones to mourn them."

"Is there anything else we can do for you, Mr. Hart?' the mortician asked.

"Yes, there is. Would you mind keeping me posted regarding the disposition of this child? If no one comes to claim the body I would very much like to legally do so myself. I will bury him in the cemetery on my property." Following a brief pause, he added, "I'll leave my home phone number with you. Please call me regarding any new developments."

"I'll certainly do that, Mr. Hart."

"One other thing: If I purchase burial clothes for the youngster, would you see to it that he is dressed in them?"

"I will, sir."

As Hart turned to go, he addressed Angela. "Thank you for what you are doing." Glancing about the room he addressed all of the volunteers. Jeff's fellow volunteers were also present in the large room, for word had gotten out that William S. Hart was making a special appearance in the morgue. "I would like to commend all of you. You are truly dedicated individuals, and I am honored to be in your presence."

Hart then turned and moved toward the front door, where Biscailuz was standing. The actor stopped long enough to write down his phone number and hand it to Oscar, then the undersheriff opened the door and the two men departed.

When they were seated in the car, Hart turned toward the undersheriff and said, "By this time I hope you don't mind if I call you Gene."

Biscailuz grinned. "Not at all. In fact, I prefer it."

"I was wondering … Gene … if I could persuade you to be the guest at my house tonight. I have plenty of room, and I'm sure you'll find it more comfortable than sleeping on a cot in the sheriff's office."

The grin widened as Gene replied, "I would be honored to stay at your house."

SHORTLY AFTER DARK Oscar called all the workers together and announced that work for the day was finished.

"What if other stiffs are brought in during the night?" High Pockets asked.

Oscar winced at the crude inquiry. "After dark the sheriff's deputies continue patrolling the area in search of live victims. It is too dark to go in search of fatalities. For this reason, we can shut down until daylight tomorrow. I suggest we all go home and get a good night's sleep, because I suspect it'll be another day much like today.

Within minutes the workers departed, except for Jeff, Angela and Oscar. Oscar studied them briefly before asking, "What's wrong? Don't the two of you have homes?"

"We're not from around here," Jeff replied. "We live up in Bishop."

"Didn't you make plans for staying over?"

"Oscar, we haven't had a single moment to plan anything. No sooner had we reported to the sheriff's station than we were sent here to work in the mortuary."

Oscar scratched his head as he studied the situation. "Unfortunately, I doubt very seriously that you will find a place to stay anywhere around here. This is a disaster area." He paused for a moment, then a smile appeared on his face. "I live in Sylmar, about ten miles from here. There's a chance that you might find a motor hotel somewhere in that area. If you're interested, I can drive you there in my car. Once you find a place, I can pick you up in the morning and bring you back here."

Jeff looked at Angela, who shrugged her approval, before replying. "That sounds good to us."

Fifteen minutes later they were on the road to Sylmar. "I would invite you to stay at my house" Oscar said. "It's just the wife and me. Unfortunately, it's a small place, with only one bedroom."

"That's quite all right," Jeff replied. "We don't want to put you out." Offering a smile, he added, "Just don't forget to pick us up in the morning."

Before arriving at the motor court Jeff asked Oscar to drive them to a local Western Union office. The young couple wanted to send a telegram to their parents, assuring them that they were safe, and would probably be gone for the next week to ten days.

Twenty minutes later, the telegrams having been sent, Oscar dropped the couple off at a modest motor court. After being assured that they each were successful in getting a room, he departed. He had informed them that he would pick them up at five-thirty the following morning.

After registering, the couple stepped outside the office and were walking toward the cottages that, fortunately, were next to one another, when Jeff suddenly stopped. Snapping his fingers, he said, "Darn it!"

"What's wrong?" Angela asked.

"It just dawned on me! We forgot to bring a change of clothes! The bags are back at the plane."

"Oh, no!" Angela replied. "What are we going to do?"

"Nothing we can do right now." He looked his companion up and down, as if inspecting her. "Your clothes are still clean, so you should be ok. But look at me! My pants and shirt are covered with mud." Taking in a deep breath, he blew it out in a sigh. "Oh, well, there's nothing we can do about it now." I'll see if I can get Oscar to run us by the airfield first thing in the morning. It's not too far out of the way. We'll take our change of clothes with us to work tomorrow." He paused as another thought occurred to him. "While we're at the airfield I want to touch base with Geri and see if we can leave the plane at her place for the next several days."

After kissing one another good night, they each proceeded to their individual cottage. An hour after Jeff got into bed he was still awake. Thoughts of all the death and destruction he had witnessed troubled him personally. His mind kept going back to something his Uncle Emmett had told him back when the older man was going through his brief and unsuccessful attempt at becoming a preacher. He had referred to Los Angeles as a modern-day Babylon, a godless place mentioned in the Bible. According to Emmett, the arrival of the movie industry brought with it a wave of sin, scantily clad women with no morals, excessive use of alcohol and a style of rich living.

After witnessing all the death during the day and realizing that he had seen only a small part of the carnage, it occurred to him that his uncle might well be guilty of mass murder.

As he lay in bed he recalled a conversation with his father. When Jeff repeated to his father what his uncle had said, his father replied that Los Angeles was no different than any other city in the country.

"It did, however, seem to be attracted to a more lavish lifestyle," Frank Kienast had said. "Home owners did manage to focus on lush lawns, which required a great amount of watering. There were also numerous homes in the city with swimming pools. I must say, though, that I seriously doubt if the movie industry had any influence in this regard." Jeff's father did concede, however, that there should probably be restrictions on the use of water – especially in a place where water had to be imported from another part of the state.

"I appreciate all this, Dad," Jeff had replied, "but what about Uncle Emmett's history of sabotaging the aqueduct?"

Jeff recalled his dad offering a patient smile. "There's a big difference between causing minor damage to the aqueduct, where no one was in danger of being harmed. Destroying a huge dam where hundreds of people are at risk of being killed is something else entirely."

The conversation, Jeff recalled, had given him comfort. The fact was, however, the dam did break, and hundreds of people had been killed. But as he lay in bed he forced himself to focus on the hope that his dad was right. Emmett Hollister was not a very nice person, but Frank found it hard to believe that his brother-in-law was a cold-blooded murderer. Having decided to focus on the words of his father, a few minutes later he was sound asleep.

THE DAYS THAT followed were much the same as the first day. They were both relieved, at the end of the second day, to return to their cottages, where each took a long bath, then changed into fresh clothing, inside and out.

During a lunch break on the third day the couple found a clothing store that had managed to stay open, where they purchased additional attire. At the end of each shift, they washed the clothes they had worn that day.

Geri, who had grown fond of the young couple, agreed to let Jeff keep his plane at her place. At his inquiry, she assured him that he could purchase enough fuel to get them safely to Mojave. This was a load off Jeff's mind.

29

MARGARET MEADOWS STARED sullenly at the mud that was a foot deep in her living room. The foul odor was almost more than she could bear. Her modest, five-room dwelling sat inside the southeastern edge of the flood zone near Saugus. Hers had been one of the many houses in the neighborhood that had suffered an assault of thick, foul-smelling mud throughout the structure.

It seemed to Margaret that she had been shoveling the slush and tossing it out the front door for hours and had seen virtually no progress. The muddy ground on which she tossed the refuse had, a few days before, been a beautiful, neatly manicured lawn, but was now part of the liquid stench that permeated the entire area.

Leaning defeatedly on the shovel, she breathed a despondent sigh. Anger began to swell within her as she thought of that dam up in Francisquito Canyon, and the terrible disaster it had wrought. Her thoughts then wandered to the man who was responsible for this sudden hell on earth – Mulholland!

Her thoughts of the man rapidly turned to hatred. He needed to pay for the disaster he had wrought on the citizens whose lives had been turned upside down.

As these thoughts ran angrily through her mind an idea began to form. Dropping the shovel onto the mud that had been her floor, Margaret waded to a back room, where she found a large piece of cardboard, four feet square. She then made her way to the detached single-car garage, where she found a small can of black paint and a half-inch wide paint brush. Setting the cardboard on a workbench, she began painting a sign. Then, with a hammer and nails, she proceeded to wade out to the fence that was partially standing in front of her house. With angry determination she nailed the sign to a post.

Over the next several days motorists would slow down to read the sign. In a matter of days other signs, similarly worded, appeared throughout the Santa Clarita Valley, and soon signs began to show up in the greater Los Angeles area. The sign contained only two words, but those words reflected the anger, frustration and sense of helplessness of everyone who suffered from the tragedy. The sign simply read:

KILL MULHOLLAND!

IT TOOK SEVERAL days for the water from the deluge to recede into the river and proceed down to the ocean. Though much shallower, it would be another week or so before the Santa Clara River was back to its normal depth of a few feet.

During these days the destruction caused by the flood came into greater focus. Thousands of acres of farmland, including large orchards of orange, lemon, walnut, and avocado trees, lay on the wet ground, stripped of their limbs and leaves. They were dead, and the damage to the owners was great.

Carcasses of horses, cows, sheep, goats, dogs, cats, as well as numerous wild creatures, began to decompose, leaving strong odors that blended with the already sickening smells the river had deposited on the ground covering a distance of fifty miles.

The death toll was in the hundreds, and more bodies were being discovered each day. The dam break was already being touted as the greatest man-made disaster in California history.

Miles of cable, telephone and electric wiring, as well as rail cars, tracks, automobiles, large trucks, tractors and other heavy machinery lay where the waters had carried them. There was no trace of many houses that had been swept into the river and carried away, then broken into tiny pieces by the turbulent flow of the flood waters.

A DAY OR SO after the waters began to recede, the bus that had gone into the river following the bridge washout on the Ridge Route, was found. It was lying on its side a mile downriver from where it fell into the water. Inside the bus sixteen bodies, including the driver, were recovered.

The clothing of the victims remained on them since they had been shielded inside the bus from the vicious torrent that had carried them downstream. Their luggage had also remained in the storage compartment. This allowed the occupants of the bus to be easily identified. Since, apparently, none of the occupants were from the immediate area, without being identified some might have left friends and relatives unaware of what had happened to them.

The luggage, accompanying each of the victims, was distributed among the make-shift mortuaries in the area. Three of the bodies were delivered to the mortuary where Jeff and Angela were assigned.

There was no refrigeration in these temporary morgues, so it was essential that the next of kin be notified as soon as possible. The volunteers worked as a team to clean the cadavers and make them presentable to those who arrived to claim the body.

JEFF AND ANGELA had been working for five days when William S. Hart returned to the mortuary. He was holding a package in his hands. Oscar immediately appeared and welcomed the famous actor.

"Is the child that I pointed out to you still here?" Hart asked.

Oscar offered a solemn expression. "Yes, he is, Mr. Hart."

"Has anyone claimed the body?"

"No sir." The mortician offered a shrug. "At this point, I am sadly confident that there will be no claimants. In all probability his entire family was killed in the flood." He paused and frowned. "Apparently, the child's body was the only one among his family members to be recovered."

"Then I want to officially claim it," Hart replied as he handed the package to Oscar. "Here are some clothes I want you to dress him in."

"Yes sir!"

"I'll come back later to claim the child's remains." Following a brief pause, he added, "I intend to bury him in the cemetery on my property."

"Yes sir," Oscar repeated.

After Hart departed Oscar quickly summoned Angela and handed her the package. He repeated the actor's instructions and Angela moved to the slab where the remains of the child lay.

Oscar had made it a point to personally embalm the body, making sure that it was well preserved, ensuring the fresh appearance of the child. This was not entirely to accommodate the wishes of the famous actor. The mortician's heart had genuinely gone out to the child.

When Angela removed the contents from the bag, she was surprised to find a complete child's cowboy outfit, including hat and boots. As she examined the clothing a wave of emotion swept over her, then she set about dressing the body of the little boy.

30

BY THE END of the second week the number of bodies recovered were noticeably reduced – at least in the immediate area of the morgue to which Jeff and Angela had been assigned. That was not to say that several recoveries would not be made, but most of the fatalities were recovered in Ventura County. Many of those victims had been carried by the flood waters across the county line and deposited all along the banks of the Santa Clara River. Ventura County had also set up a number of temporary morgues, and the challenge of identifying victims fell to that county.

Jeff had given Oscar notice a few days earlier. It was time for them to head back to Bishop, and today was their last day. It was a slow day at the morgue, so Jeff and Angela spent a longer time in the break room than usual. Other volunteers had been slowly departing until the two of them were the only ones in the room.

"Angie," Jeff began, a look of reluctance on his face. "There's something I would like to ask you."

Angela grinned. "I was wondering why you've been acting so fidgety." She smiled knowingly. "Is this why you were waiting until we were alone?"

"Yes," he replied, a note of irritation in his voice.

"Well, what is it?"

"Angie," he began again, "We've known each other all of our lives. Except for the years you were away at college, we've been together almost constantly."

Angela was still in a teasing mood. "Are you trying to say you are tired of me?"

"No!" he said irritably, then softened his voice. "No, that's not what I'm saying." Following a pause, he continued, "Ever since we flew down here I've begun to look at you in a different light." He shook his head, as if groping for the right words.

Angela's teasing mood suddenly changed, and her words became softer. "Are you saying you are in love with me?"

Jeff's eyes widened. "Yes! That's what I've been trying to say!" A questioning look appeared on his face. "How did you know?"

"Because, silly, I have those same feelings about you."

"You do?" As the realization of what Angela said fully registered, Jeff became emboldened and asked, "Will you marry me?"

Angela then lost her smile and she gazed at him somberly. "Are you actually proposing to me in a morgue?"

"Huh?" he asked, a questioning expression on his face. "What difference does that make?"

"Jeff, I don't want to be proposed to in a morgue." She looked at him as if she were addressing a child. "How would we explain it to our children? How can we tell them that you waited until we were in a morgue before you asked me to marry you?"

Jeff slowly rose from his chair. "Sorry, Angie. I guess I never gave it much thought." As he turned to walk away he added, "Please forgive me."

At the end of the day Oscar drove the couple to the motor court in Sylmar. Pulling up in front of their rooms, he stopped the car and gazed at the couple he had come to regard quite fondly.

"Well, kids," he began. "Looks like this is where we part company. I want to thank you both for your valuable service." After a brief pause he added, "I think I told you that tomorrow is the last day our particular morgue will be operational. It'll take a few days to clean it out, then I can get back to my own undertaking business."

Jeff reached for the door handle, then stopped. "Oscar, I wonder if you could do one more thing for us."

"Name it."

"Could you come by tomorrow, like you have been doing, and give us a lift to the airfield?"

Oscar offered a friendly smile. "I'd be happy to."

A moment later Jeff and Angela stood outside the car and waved as Oscar drove away. Jeff glanced briefly at Angela before turning and walking toward his room. A sadness filled Angela as she watched him go.

THE FOLOWING MORNING Oscar dropped the young couple off at the airfield. He stayed only long enough to bid them both farewell and a safe flight home. Jeff then took his and Angela's bags to the plane and loaded them aboard. Angela, meanwhile, walked to the house, where she met Geri coming out the door.

"Ah, Angela, it's good to see you again."

Angela offered a sad smile. "Morning, Geri. Well, it's time for us to head back home."

Geri frowned. "I'm sorry to see you go, but I understand. The two of you, true to your word, did what you came here to do, and I reckon you're both tuckered out. I'm gonna miss you."

"We're going to miss you, too. You've been so good to us."

Geri studied the younger woman, then asked, "Are you ok, Angela? You don't look well."

Angela forced a smile. "I'm ok, Geri. I guess I'm just tired."

"Well, that's certainly natural, considering what you've been doing this past week or so." Wanting to change the subject, Geri said, "I know you're anxious to get back home, so I'll drive the tanker truck over to where Jeff's plane is, and he can refuel it without having to move it."

By the time Geri and Angela arrived in the tanker truck, Jeff had completed his pre-flight check of the aircraft. Ten minutes later the fuel tank was full. The young couple gave Geri an affectionate hug, then climbed into the Jenny.

As Jeff reached out and handed Geri the money as payment for the fuel Geri offered a sad smile. "I want you both to know that you are always welcome here. You can park your plane here anytime." Geri then moved to the front of the plane, reached up and grasped one side of the prop.

Jeff, placing both feet on the brake pedals, flipping a toggle and moving the throttle wide open, he shouted, "Contact!"

Geri pulled down hard on the prop and quickly stepped back as the engine sputtered a few seconds then became quiet. Geri moved back to the prop and Jeff shouted again, "Contact!"

Once again Geri pulled down hard on the prop before quickly moving back. The engine sputtered again, this time coming to life and roaring at full throttle.

Geri waved and moved to the tanker truck. A moment later she was driving the vehicle back to its parking space a safe distance from the house. Jeff, meanwhile, taxied the plane onto the runway. He gave it full throttle and the plane raced along the airstrip. Angela waved to Geri as they passed the front of the house. A moment later they were in the air, heading west by northwest.

An hour later the aircraft landed in Mojave. Jeff and Angela stood nearby while an employee of the motor court topped off the plane's fuel tank.

"Are you hungry?" Jeff asked.

Angela shrugged. "I didn't have any breakfast. I guess I am getting pretty hungry."

"There's a restaurant attached to this motor court." Jeff paused to shake his head. "It's not the neatest place, and I've never eaten here, but we can give it a try if you like."

Five minutes later, the plane having been refueled, the couple entered the restaurant. Except for two middle-aged men sitting across from one another in a far corner and a young couple sitting side-by-side in another corner, the place was void of customers.

An uncomfortable silence was felt by both Jeff and Angela as they quietly studied the menu. A waitress arrived and they gave their orders. When the waitress departed Angela stared across the table at Jeff and their eyes met.

"I apologize, Jeff," Angela said softly. "I know I hurt your feelings when I responded to your proposal yesterday." When Jeff made no reply, she continued, "I wasn't saying that I didn't want to marry you. I do – very much. It's just that you caught me completely off guard by proposing to me where you did – in a morgue of all places!"

Jeff made no reply at first, then a slow smile appeared on his face. "You're right. That was a stupid thing to do, and I apologize."

Returning the smile, Angela replied, "Apology accepted." Reaching across the table, she took Jeff's hand. "And I hope and pray that another proposal from you is forthcoming."

Jeff's smile broadened. "How would you like being proposed to in a less-than-elegant restaurant such as this?"

"I would be honored."

An hour later they were back in the air, heading home. The next day they would drive to Bishop and find a jewelry store, and the engagement would become official.

31

DEPUTY PAUL NESTER, following his assignment at the bridge disaster, returned to the station and was assigned routine patrol duties in the area for the next several days. By the time his ten-day tour of duty was up he and the deputies who had accompanied him to Newhall were more than ready to head back to Temple Station. While he had an affection for Newhall and the deputies who worked there, Temple City was now his home. It was also Paul Nester's home, and he had missed his wife and children.

WILLIAM S. HART and his guest, Undersheriff Eugene Biscailuz, sat in the large living room of the elegant Hart residence. It had been ten days since the undersheriff arrived at the Newhall Sheriff's Station. That first night he had accepted an invitation to spend the night at the actor's home. Though he decided to spend the remaining days with his deputies at the station, his brief encounter with Hart had been a pleasant experience. On his last day in the Newhall area, he felt obligated to pay the former actor another visit and convey his sincere appreciation for Hart's kindness.

Gene sipped the coffee that had been served him as he took in the actor's large living room. It was twenty-four feet wide by forty-eight feet long, beneath a twelve-foot ceiling. In one corner sat a brand new Chickering piano, the top of which was graced by a wood carving of a stagecoach and a team of six horses, by Gene Hoback. On the walls were a number of paintings, all with western themes, by such luminaries as Charles M. Russell, James Montgomery Flagg and Frederick Remington. On the floor near the fireplace was a huge bear rug, a gift from Hart's close friend, Will Rogers.

"You sure have a wonderful home, Bill," the undersheriff observed.

"Thank you, Gene. It's a lifetime collection. Each piece in here tells a story, and I wouldn't part with them for anything."

On other walls throughout the elegant home were numerous items of memorabilia, including photos of Hart with such notables as Mary Pickford, Will Rogers, Wyatt Earp, Bat Masterson, Cecil B. DeMille, Charles Russell and many others.

Gene set his coffee cup on the table. "I'm curious, Bill. It just occurred to me that one of your contemporaries lives quite close to you, yet I haven't seen any photos of him."

"Who might that be?" the actor asked.

"A few miles north of here is the Harry Carey Ranch. Until you retired, Carey, Tom Mix and you were the foremost western actors in the business."

The undersheriff paused before pursuing his question. "I guess what I'm saying is that I took it for granted that the three of you would be close acquaintances."

"We are close acquaintances. I like both Tom and Harry. Tom is a self-promoter and is always on the go. As for Harry ..." he paused briefly, as if searching for the right words. "Harry is a good man, and at one time we were quite close."

Gene sensed that he had hit on a tender spot, so he was about to change the subject when Hart continued. "For a brief period in my life I was married. It was in late 1921 I made a movie called "John Petticoats." My co-star was Winnifred Westover. Despite our age difference we decided to get married – she was twenty-one and I was fifty-seven." Hart tried to force a smile. "But anyone with eyes could see that the marriage wouldn't last. Five months later we separated." He paused again to take a deep breath. "She happened to be pregnant at the time. Four months later she gave birth to a son. She named him William S. Hart, Jr.

"While I was unhappy about her leaving me, I was elated by the fact that she had borne me a son – the only child I will ever have. Unfortunately, she would seldom let me see him, yet she remained legally married to me for the next five years. It wasn't until last year that she took a trip to Reno, Nevada and obtained a divorce."

Hart offered a humorless grin. "Now, you may be wondering what this has to do with Harry Carey and me. Well, it happened that Harry Carey's wife, Olive Carey, who is also a well-known actress, happens to be a close friend of Winnifred." Hart shook his head. "Lord only knows what Winnifred has filled Olive's head with." Hart looked in Gene's eyes. "As God is my witness, I have never done anything to harm her or our son. But I'm sure that's not the story Olive has heard. She refuses to have anything to do with me.

"There is nothing bad between Harry and me, but, needless to say, Olive's hard feelings toward me has put Harry in an awkward position. As far as our friendship goes, he's been placed between a rock and a hard spot."

Following another deep sigh, Hart concluded, "Oh, well. Enough of that. What do you say we step out to the corral, and you can say 'farewell' to Fritz, the greatest horse in the movies." Fritz was the pinto that William S. Hart rode in most of his movies. The undersheriff had met Fritz on his first visit to the Hart ranch ten days earlier. But he knew that the horse was very special to Hart, and he was not about to turn down the invitation.

After the visit to the corral Hart walked the undersheriff back up the hill to the driveway where Gene's car was parked. As he was getting into the car, the undersheriff stopped when his host said, "Gene, I would appreciate it if you wouldn't repeat what I said about Harry Carey. He's a great guy, and I wouldn't want any of this to get out."

Gene offered a sympathetic grin. "You have my word." The undersheriff started the car and made his way down the driveway toward the road that would take him back to the sheriff's station. He would pick up his companions and head back home. The Undersheriff missed his family. It had been a long ten days.

VII:
REVELATION
AND
REMORSE
1928

32

IN THE DAYS and weeks following the disaster the city of Los Angeles dispatched a number of uniformed officers of the Los Angeles Police Department into Ventura County to assist in rescue and recovery. Ventura County residents, however, rejected their help. They had nothing against the officers per se. They simply did not want anything to do with the city of Los Angeles short of complete monetary restitution for the damage suffered. The officers conducted themselves professionally and proved to be of great assistance in aiding the victims. Soon the attitudes of the Ventura County residents changed, and the assistance of L.A.P.D. was gladly accepted.

There was one entity that came into the county that proved to be damaging to many of the citizens. A wave of personal injury lawyers began drifting in from all over the state. These were members of the bar that gave the legal profession a bad name. They were known as ambulance chasers. Many of the flood victims, however, welcomed these interlopers, for they were assured of a speedy payment for their losses. Unfortunately, the money they received for damages were but a pittance of what they would have received by having the patience to wait for the legal issues to run their course through the courts. Sadly, signing an agreement with these unsavory members of the bar precluded the victims from further legal remedy.

An organization that proved to be of genuine assistance to the victims of the flood was the American Red Cross. Within days the Red Cross was providing aid such as food, clothing, household furnishings, and even assisted in the care of the farm animals by offering money for feed and farm equipment.

HARVEY VAN NORMAN arrived in Ventura County, representing the Los Angeles Water Company. The company had taken part in an enormous operation to clean up and repair the damage caused by the flood. The actual work would be undertaken by the Associated General Contractors. Local contractors, working under the umbrella of Associated General, would provide manpower, made up of workers who actually lived in the areas needing the work. A total of four base camps were set up stretching from Piru to Santa Paula. Between forty to one hundred men were assigned to each camp, depending upon the extent of damage at any particular area. Each camp was provided with eight caterpillar tractors, clamshells, a back filler, service trucks, a burning outfit and a blacksmith shop. The number of each piece of equipment depended upon the size of the area being cleaned up.

The largest town in the area was Santa Paula, and it was here that Harvey Van Norman made his headquarters. During his first few days in the colorful town, he made it a point to meet various officials to gain input on the mood of the community. He spoke with police and fire officials, as well as other prominent members of the town. The one person with whom he most enjoyed conversing was Officer Thornton Edwards. He found Edwards to be eloquent, knowledgeable and, to Van Norman's delight, gifted with a sense of humor. This was in spite of the fact that Edwards and his small family had lost most of their possessions in the flood, including their home. But the young officer never once revealed any attitude of self-pity or resentment.

It was Edwards who had recommended the Glen Tavern to Van Norman. This was a local establishment that offered a quiet, peaceful setting where a person could go and enjoy a nice drink while sitting near a warm fireplace. It was one of a few establishments in the area that revenue agents seemed to overlook.

One evening, after the engineer had taken a seat beside the fireplace, and just as a waiter was setting a class of brandy on the table near him the door opened, and the loud voice of a man entered. Van Norman noticed a frown appear on the waiter's face.

"Who is that?" Van Norman asked.

The waiter breathed a deep sigh. "That, sir, is the irrepressible Hee Haw."

"Excuse me?" Van Norman's words were barely out when a loud "Haw Haw" echoed through the bar.

"And that is why we call him Hee Haw," The waiter added.

"Who is he?"

"He's a traveling salesman. Every few weeks he comes through Santa Paula and stops in here for a drink and to pass along the latest corny jokes he has heard since his last trip. He always finishes his punch line with that annoying guffaw."

The bartender turned to walk away, then stopped and faced his customer. "By the way, he likes to sit by the fire."

Just as Van Norman was opening his newspaper to begin reading, the loud patron appeared, then stopped upon seeing someone else in his chair. Giving Van Norman an unfriendly glare, he reached behind him and pulled a chair from a nearby table and placed it in front of the fireplace. He sat down hard, spilling some of his drink. The engineer acknowledged the man's presence, then resumed reading his paper.

"Are you part of this clean-up operation that's going on around here?" the man asked.

Van Norman set his paper aside. "Yes, I am."

"I heard one of the craziest stories recently about that dam that broke and caused all this damage."

"Oh? What did you hear?" It was more of an obligatory response than interest in anything the man might have to say.

"This man tried to tell me that there would have been just as much pressure against the wall of the dam if there was only four feet of water pressing against it instead of four miles. Isn't that the craziest thing you ever heard?"

"Actually, there is quite a bit of truth in what the man said." Van Norman replied.

Taken aback, Hee Haw glared at the man who had uttered those words. "What's your name, Mister?

"My name is Harvey Van Norman."

"What makes you an authority?"

"I'm an engineer for the Los Angeles Water Company."

"Did you have anything to do with that dam that just busted?"

"Yes, I did."

"Well, I'm not surprised. No wonder the damn thing broke." The comment was followed by another loud "Haw Haw!"

Rather than get into a deeper discussion regarding the laws of physics, Van Norman arose, took the last drink from his glass, left a tip for the waiter, then departed. He would make a few more trips to the Glen Tavern over the next several weeks, and to his relief he would not encounter Hee Haw.

Eventually, the clean-up project was completed, and Harvey Van Norman returned to his office at the water company.

DURING THE WEEKS and months following the disaster Bill Mulholland maintained the routine of going to his office each day, though the symptoms of shock and depression were apparent to those who were close to him. On more than one occasion Harvey Van Norman, back from his duties in Santa Paula and having assumed many of the duties that would normally be handled by the Chief, would step into Mulholland's office and find the Old Man, his chair facing away from the huge desk and toward the window, staring out at seemingly nothing. His face would be expressionless, and it was impossible to know what kind of hell was going through the Old Man's mind. Yet Mulholland hung in there, day after day.

Van Norman was fully aware that the boss had seen the 'Kill Mulholland' signs that were springing up throughout the county. One sign had been placed in Mulholland's own neighborhood to make sure the boss saw it. Van Norman was incensed by the act, and quickly arranged to have the sign removed.

Until the dam disaster William Mulholland was regarded as one of the foremost hydraulic engineers in the United States. The aqueduct, stretching from Owens Valley to Los Angeles – a distance of two hundred forty miles, much of it having been tunneled through several miles of the Tehachapi Mountains, ranked among the great engineering feats of the twentieth century. He had been recruited to serve as a consultant on the construction of the Colorado River's Boulder Dam. But now he was persona non grata, due primarily to the fact that the dam construction project had yet to be approved by the federal government. Of necessity, Mulholland's name now had to be removed as a prominent player in the project.

Though he retained his position as head of the water company, many associates who had once clamored to gain the attention of the famous engineer now made excuses to avoid him. There were others, however, who steadfastly stood by their leader. Foremost among them was Harvey Van Norman. He felt the need to protect his boss from public humiliation, for he had worked alongside Mulholland, and was aware of the pains he had taken to ensure that the dam was constructed in the safest way possible. Like his boss, Van Norman was at a complete loss as to what caused the disaster. He was also fully aware that the tragedy was taking a heavy toll on his friend and superior.

During Van Norman's numerous visits to the boss's office, several 'what if' questions were posed by the Chief. Uppermost among these involved his former friend, Fred Eaton. He wondered, numerous times, what might have happened if he had gone along with his former friend and acquiesced to the purchase of Eaton's property in Owens Valley. This would have included the deep canyon north of Bishop that Mulholland had originally hoped to be used as the reservoir. In addition to providing water for the farmers in Owens Valley, there would have been more than enough to supplant the needs of the residents of Los Angeles during periods of drought. It was the decision to forego this purchase from Eaton that had led Mulholland to search elsewhere for a reservoir, and Francisquito Canyon was the result of that search. In retrospect, Mulholland's sense of ethics might have been misplaced. After all, Fred Eaton was asking only one million dollars for the property. It proved to be a pittance compared to the many millions the city would have to pay the victims of the flood disaster.

These were among the 'what if' questions Mulholland posed to himself every day following the disaster. Harvey Van Norman was aware that these thoughts were slowly killing his boss.

33

NINE DAYS AFTER the catastrophe occurred a coroner's inquest convened. Friends of Tony Harnischfeger testified that Tony was quite worried about the safety of the dam. He was known to make remarks such as "I'll see you tomorrow ... if the dam doesn't break." There was testimony by others who related similar concerns by Mr. Harnischfeger.

One thing that appeared strange about Tony's fear of the dam collapsing was the fact that he lived in a small cottage at the bottom of the canyon a mere quarter of a mile downstream from the dam. He lived there with his common law wife and seven-year-old son. If his concern about the dam breaking was as serious as he seemed to express it to his friends, why would he continue to live in such a vulnerable location? If the dam broke while he was inside the house, it would have been impossible for him or his family to escape before the deluge was upon them. While it is likely that his concerns were genuine, they were not strong enough to prompt him to move his family to a safer location. This might leave a disinterested third party to conclude that Tony really had nothing to go on to convince him that the dam was ready to break at any moment.

When Tony had requested Mr. Mulholland to visit the dam on the morning of the disaster, the leaks that Tony pointed out to Mr. Mulholland and Mr. Van Norman were checked out, and neither of them had anything to do with the actual breaking of the dam. All dams leaked to some degree but were not regarded as dangerous, as long as the water was clear. Still, the fact remains that the dam did, in fact, collapse. What caused it?

Mulholland was of the opinion that the dam might have been dynamited. A careful inspection of the area at and around the dam site, however, failed to reveal any trace of dynamite.

There were accusations that the dam had been constructed with dirty, substandard concrete, and bed springs had been used for reinforcing the concrete. Stories about numerous leaks leading to the dam's collapse were rampant. Every one of these accusations were disproved. The fact was that high quality concrete was used and was reinforced by approved steel rebar.

When Mulholland's turn came to testify he slowly stood and several in the room, having only now seen him for the first time since the tragic incident, were appalled by his appearance. The man seemed to have aged several years in the past few weeks.

When he spoke, his words came out pained and sad. He said, "Don't blame anyone else, you just fasten it on me. If there was an error in human judgement, I was the human, and I won't try to fasten it on anyone else." Following a brief pause, he added, "On occasions like this, I envy the dead."

After several weeks of interviews and testimony, the inquest cleared Mulholland of any charges, but added that "the construction and operation of a great dam should never be left to the sole judgment of one man, no matter how eminent."

The commission concluded that the failure of the dam was due to defective foundations. There were those, however, who insisted on blaming Mulholland, accusing him of arrogance and a lack of formal engineering training.

During the course of the inquest Mulholland offered to resign as chief engineer but the board refused to accept his resignation, replying, "The board hereby declines to grant such a request and urges the chief to remain on the job he has so faithfully filled for half a century."

EPILOGUE

THE CHAUFFEUR TURNED west onto a street in downtown Los Angeles. In his camera were the still undeveloped photographs that he had taken three months earlier atop the dam. In time, those photos would make their way onto the pages of magazines, newspapers and books. They were the last photographs taken of the dam before its collapse. It is unknown if the photos ever provided the chauffeur with any sizable income, but it is certainly probable that the pictures were released with the Chief's approval.

In the back seat William Mulholland sat alone. Harvey Van Norman had offered to accompany the boss on this trip, but he was told that this was a very personal excursion that he preferred to make alone.

While Mulholland was still the titular head of the Department, the fact was that Van Norman was running the day-to-day operations. The old Chief was actually looking for things to keep him busy, and this is what led him to make an excursion on this day.

At Mulholland's direction, the chauffeur made his way to the area of the Los Angeles River, then proceeded west. The old Plaza and the Pico House were the only points of reference he recalled from the early days. Almost everything west of the Plaza was changed. The remainder of the outing would be much more difficult.

When he first arrived in Los Angeles in 1877 the population was nine thousand. Fifty years later it had climbed to 2.1 million. The size of the downtown part of the city had grown proportionately. The location of his first work assignment as a deputy *zanjero* was now part of the business section of the city. The *zanja*, or ditch, where he had worked was no longer there, having long since been filled in and was now probably under a street, or a row of houses. The object of his search would not be in a better part of town, but it would certainly be well populated.

Driving in a westerly direction from the river Mulholland scanned the neighborhoods, looking for the slightest landmark that would assure him that they were on the right track. After an hour of driving up and down streets, while maintaining a generally western direction, they came upon an open area that caught Mulholland's eye, and he directed the chauffeur to stop.

The driver exited the car then opened the back door, and Mulholland stepped out. As he looked about he found himself standing in a large vacant field, surrounded by houses and small buildings. For some reason, where he stood had not yet been developed.

Several feet north of him was the burned-out ruins of a modest structure. The concrete foundation frame was still in place, and outlined what might well have been the tiny residence where he had lived during his earliest *zanjero* days. He had not expected to find the structure still standing, but just looking at the concrete foundation outline brought back fond memories.

His mind raced back to his many days, weeks and months of studying courses in a variety of subjects related to engineering inside the tiny dwelling. These were fond memories. Then, suddenly, another special memory came into focus. It was the day his friend, Sheriff Henry Mitchell, paid him a visit. Mitchell was the first person he and brother Hugh met on their first day in Los Angeles. He took a liking to the young newcomers, and they had taken an instant liking to him. Soon afterward Hugh departed for places unknown, but William and Henry remained friends for several years – until the tragic and untimely death of the former sheriff.

Mulholland unconsciously smiled as he wondered how proud Henry might have been to see how far the poor *zanjero* would rise in the business of bringing water to the city. Then a frown replaced the smile when he was reminded of the sad ending of the self-made engineer's career. Tears flowed and he turned his back so the chauffeur could not see his face. As he wiped the wetness away with a handkerchief a relief came over him as he thought of how grateful he was that Henry Mitchell was not around to see his protégé's downfall.

Turning toward the open ground, Mulholland noticed, for the first time, the two trees standing near one another. The first was a sycamore, and it stood at least sixty feet high, with a spread of limbs that encircled the trunk twenty-five feet in diameter. To the west of the tree was a live oak – not as tall as the sycamore, nor did the limbs extend quite so far, but it revealed all the characteristics of a sturdy oak, standing thirty feet high.

Again, thoughts of Henry Mitchell flooded his mind, but now they were happy thoughts. He recalled again the day of Sheriff Mitchell's visit. William had planted the oak sapling near the sycamore, and Mitchell suggested that he move it several feet away. Had he not heeded the sheriff's advice, the oak probably would not have taken root.

For a brief moment Bill Mulholland thought of seeking the owner of this property and possibly purchasing it. It would be a pleasant place for him to visit, perhaps construct a small cottage at the spot of the ruins of his old abode.

It was a pleasant thought, but then the reality struck home. William Mulholland's health was failing him, and he knew that he was not long for this world. The stress and strain of recent events had taken its toll. He was aware of the comments, uttered in whispers as he passed along the corridors at work, describing his aged appearance. The stress was killing him, and he would probably never see these trees again.

Five minutes later the chauffeur-driven vehicle was heading back to the office.

WILLIAM MULHOLLAND WOULD live a few more years as his health continued to decline. Following his official retirement he lived in seclusion, his oldest daughter tending to his needs. During his last days he endeavored to write his autobiography. However, his health was deteriorating rapidly, and he was forced to abandon the project, knowing full well that he would not be able to complete it. On July 22, 1935, following a stroke, the man who brought water from hundreds of miles away and quenched the thirst of a growing metropolis, quietly passed away – less than two months shy of his eightieth birthday.

A year earlier, on March 11, 1934, his former friend and colleague, Fred Eaton, died. Despite their differences, both men contributed significantly to bringing water to Los Angeles. When thinking of Eaton, Mulholland must surely have experienced momentary regret at refusing to back his former friend in selling Eaton's property in Owens Valley. Had Mulholland acquiesced to the purchase of that property by the city of Los Angeles, the dam would have been built north of Bishop, in a very sparsely populated area, and there would never have been a dam in San Francisquito Canyon, and this disaster would never have occurred. Nevertheless, William Mulholland's deeper sense of ethical conduct would not have allowed him to take any other action than what he did take. Despite the terrible tragedy, William Mulholland would go to his grave well aware that he had done the right thing.

From a tiny community of nine thousand inhabitants in 1877, by the end of the twentieth century Los Angeles would grow to become the second largest city in the United States, and to this day water must be imported from sources miles away. The aqueduct, built by Mulholland over a century ago, is still a major conveyance for hauling that water. Without the vision and efforts of William Mulholland and his colleague, Fred Eaton, the water issues might well have been the cause of a different fate for the City of Angeles.

AUTHOR'S
NOTES

A LAYMAN'S OBSERVATIONS

In 1995, sixty-eight years after the St. Francis Dam disaster, a geological engineer related that the dam had, in fact, been partially constructed atop an ancient landslide. The weight of the dam caused the landslide to shift, resulting in the dam's collapse. It should be noted that technology, in the 1920s, was not available to allow any engineer – or geologist – of the time to have any knowledge of the huge ancient landslide. As far as Mulholland, or any engineer in the 1920s was aware, the site chosen for the dam was quite safe.

Sometime during construction, Mulholland made the decision to raise the height of the dam several feet, taking it to a height of 180 feet above the canyon floor. Contemporary argument contends that the added weight is what brought pressure on the ancient landslide, causing the structure to collapse. A question one might ask is this: If the height of the dam, as originally planned, which created an enormous weight atop the landslide, would probably have caused the dam's collapse, would that not make the additional height of the dam a moot point? It would seem that the presence of the landslide, in any case, would have caused the structure to collapse. Of course, this is all speculation offered by the author, who is neither an engineer nor a geologist – merely a layman who claims at least a modicum of common sense.

It should also be noted that Mulholland was not the only engineer involved in the construction of the dam or the building of the aqueduct. There were other engineers on sight who were intimately aware of every phase of the construction. Of course, it was Mulholland who always had the final say in issues relating to the dam. To the best of this writer's knowledge, none of these engineers ever challenged the idea of adding extra weight to the top of the dam, nor did these college educated engineers discuss the remote possibility of a geologic phenomenon existing deep underground that might be a threat to the stability of the structure. This was because the ancient landslide was unknown to everyone. It is always easier to make judgements after the fact.

It should also be pointed out that the construction of the dam was not the most significant of Mulholland's accomplishments. That honor goes to the construction of the Owens Valley Aqueduct. The development of a massive water conveyance system 230 miles across a desert, through a range of mountains and across an earthquake fault to deliver a precious commodity to a thirsty populous was nothing less than phenomenal. This, above all others, is the feat for which William Mulholland should be remembered.

Why am I making these points? To reveal the love and dedication Mulholland poured out of his life to accomplish all that he did for Los Angeles. For fifty years he dedicated most of every waking hour to the interests of the city, particularly where water was concerned. Without his contributions, Los Angeles would never have grown into the city that it is today.

SEPARATING FACT FROM FICTION

A reminder to the reader that this is a work of fiction, based upon true events. While most of the characters are quite real (especially those responding to the dam collapse, as well as the known victims), there are others who are fictional. They are there to move the story along in an entertaining manner, and do not alter the actual tragedy in any way. It should be pointed out, however, that, with regard to the woman who painted the "Kill Mulholland" sign, while this is a true story, the name of the person is fictitious.

Another example of mixing fact with fiction was the friendship between Bill Mulholland and Sheriff Henry Mitchell. While both of these men were contemporaries, and quite likely knew one another, the friendship described in the story is fictional. It should be noted, however, that the law enforcement exploits of Mitchell, relating to the capture of both Tiburcio Vasques and Miguel Sotello, is quite true. Deputy Adolf Celis, who assisted Sheriff Mitchel in the capture of Sotello, was also a real person, and highly esteemed as a lawman.

Among the fictional characters are Jeff Kienast, Angela Lundstrum, Emmett Hollister, Frank Kienast, Geraldine (Gerty) Summers, and Oscar Reynolds, the mortician. Christopher Boswell, one of the workers at the Edison camp, is fictional, as is the unnamed friend of Mulholland (whose comments are presented in italics). The purpose of these players was to bring the story into greater focus. The vast majority of the men and women described in this story, however, are quite real. Their experiences are factual and are a matter of record.

PROMINENT PLAYERS IN THE RESCUE / RECOVERY EFFORT AND THEIR LIVES AFTER THE DISASTER

WILLIAM S. HART

William S. Hart was already retired from acting at the time of the dam disaster. He retired in 1925 after completing his last film, *Tumbleweed*. This was also, arguably, his best picture. Mr. Hart would live the remainder of his life at his Newhall ranch.

The morning following the flood, Hart and Biscailuz did meet, and they did, in fact, ride together in the undersheriff's car, inspecting the damage caused by the flood. That evening Biscailuz did spend the night at Hart's home. The last day of the undersheriff's tour of the area, however, when he visited Hart, is fiction.

His gesture of providing a cowboy outfit for a small unidentified boy who was killed in the flood is also quite true.

Hart would spend his retirement years, in part, writing children's books – mostly novels. He also wrote an autobiography entitled *My Life East and West*. Mr. Hart passed away on June 23, 1946, at the age of 81.

EUGENE BISCAILUZ

Shortly after returning home from the dam disaster Eugene Biscailuz was summoned to Sacramento by the governor to organize the state's Highway Patrol. Until the establishment of the California Highway Patrol there had been motorcycle patrolmen, associated with the state but assigned to the cities that paid their salary. Thornton Edwards was among those patrolmen.

It was the task of Biscailuz to assemble an organization that would focus strictly on traffic matters and would be completely run by the state of California. It was a tremendous challenge, but he was up to it. The job took eighteen months.

Afterward, Biscailuz returned to Los Angeles and was soon reinstated to his former post of Undersheriff. In 1932 Los Angeles County Sheriff William Traeger, having been elected to Congress, resigned his post as sheriff. A month later the Board of Supervisors appointed Gene Biscailuz to replace him.

The Sheriff appointed his old friend, Captain Arthur Jewel, to the rank of Undersheriff. One of the first acts of the new undersheriff, in all probability, must surely have been to remind the sheriff of their conversation following the dam break regarding the issuing of uniforms for the deputies.

The machinery involved in the issuing of uniforms was still in the works a year later, when southern California was hit with a huge earthquake. The source of the quake was the Newport-Inglewood Fault, extending from Culver City to Newport Beach, then veering west, into the Pacific Ocean. Commonly referred to as the Long Beach Earthquake, it destroyed business structures, schools and houses along the coast for more than forty miles.

Assistance from every fire department and law enforcement agency in the region was requested. The Los Angeles County Sheriff's Office was prominent among those that responded. Like the St. Francis Dam disaster five years earlier, the task of rescue, recovery and restoring to order took several weeks. Once more it revealed the need for law enforcement representatives to be easily recognized. Soon afterward, patrol deputies in Los Angeles County were easily identified by their uniforms.

Eugene Biscailuz would hold the office of Sheriff for twenty-six years, retiring in 1958.

THORNTON EDWARDS

As the days following the disaster turned into weeks, and counts were made of persons lost and saved, it became common knowledge that Officer Thornton Edwards personally saved over one hundred lives. With siren blaring, he had ridden up and down residential streets, awaking people and advising them of the impending danger. After other police arrived, accompanied by the fire department, he was free to proceed to Willard Bridge, where he was credited with removing as many as one hundred men, women and children off the bridge and away from the river. He would soon be given the moniker "the Paul Revere of the St. Francis Dam Disaster."

The popularity of motorcycle officer Thornton Edwards endeared him to the citizens of Santa Paula, California. In 1929, a year after the flood, he was appointed Chief of Police of Santa Paula, and would hold that position for ten years.

In 1939 he moved his family to Inglewood, a community south of Los Angeles, about eight miles east of the Pacific Ocean. Here, he opened a cabinet making business. He purchased the building and, with Ethel's consent, constructed a house on the property. At this time Thornton, Jr. was a grown man of twenty-one, and was serving a tour of duty in the Navy.

The business was soon doing very well, and it was about this time that Thornton began to get the itch to go back to making movies. The movies were now talkies, and salaries were considerably higher than what he had experienced during the silent days.

The cabinet making business proved to be a financial success, and he had a few craftsmen working for him. When he confessed to Ethel his desire to give movie acting another try, she gave him her blessing. She was comforted by the fact that the cabinet business would provide a comfortable income for them in the event Thornton's acting quest did not pan out.

Thornton was now in his forties, and the years were beginning to show. Though he still had a full head of dark hair, he had put on several pounds over the past ten years and was fully aware that he was not leading man material. The parts he would try out for would be supporting roles.

He still sported a thick, black mustache. While his grasp of the Spanish language left a great deal to be desired, Thornton seemed to have perfected the dialect. This would prove to be quite helpful, since the vast majority of parts he would play over the years were that of a Latino – particularly a Mexican.

One of his first appearances in a talkie was the part of a motorcycle cop in *The Grapes of Wrath* (1940). This was an Academy Award winning production directed by John Ford. Unfortunately, Thornton's appearance was so brief, if one blinked, they would miss him.

Later that year he appeared in a Hopalong Cassidy movie entitled *Three Men From Texas*. In this movie he had a significant part, as a Mexican outlaw, and he was quite good. In 1941 he was cast in a Gene Autry feature, entitled *Down Mexico Way*. His part was that of Rurale Captain Rodriguez. This was a good year for Thornton, for he appeared in no fewer than ten movies.

WHEN THE JAPANESE bombed Pearl Harbor on December 7, 1941, Thornton's life took a dramatic turn. His son, Thornton, Jr., was still in the Navy, stationed aboard the *USS Yorktown (CV-5)*. In June 1942, during the Battle of Midway, the *Yorktown* was sunk by a Japanese submarine. Thankfully, Thornton Jr. was among the survivors.

This had a devastating impact on Thornton and Ethel, having almost lost their only son. At the age of forty-eight, Thornton took a hiatus from the movies and enlisted in the Navy. His hope was to join his son wherever his new assignment might be. As it turned out, however, the Navy would not put father and son together, and Thornton, Sr., with his police background, was assigned to shore patrol duty. He would remain in the Navy for the duration, having attained the rate of chief petty officer.

After the war Thornton returned to movie making and appeared in several more features between 1945 and 1949. He retired at age fifty-five, having appeared in a total of twenty-five talkies and eleven silents.

IN 1978 J. J. O'BRIEN, a retired lieutenant of the California Highway Patrol, organized a fifty-year reunion of the St. Francis Dam disaster survivors. During the reunion Lt. O'Brien awarded Thornton Edwards a plaque, which read: "Conspicuous Bravery for actions taken on March 13, 1928."

It was the first such honor presented by the California Highway Patrol. There have been many more since.

Thornton Edwards would live another ten years after receiving the award from C.H.P., passing away on February 1, 1988, at age 93. He was survived by his loving wife, Ethel, and son, Thornton, Jr. Ethel would pass away on June 18, 1993, at age 98. Thornton Jr. was 75 years old when his mother passed away.

HARVEY VAN NORMAN

In 1929 Harvey Van Norman succeeded William Mulholland as Chief Engineer and General Manager of the Bureau of Water Works and Supply. He would hold this position until 1943, when the bureaus of water and power merged. At that time Van Norman was appointed General Manager and Chief Engineer of the entire Department. Its name was changed to the Los Angeles Department of Water and Power. He was well liked and respected by all who knew him.

Van Norman passed away on January 16, 1954, forty-seven years after he began employment with the water department. He was 75 years of age.

LOUISE GIPE

Louise Gipe, the night phone operator, who had called Thornton Edwards earlier to advise him of the impending disaster, had remained at her post throughout the entire night, notifying police, fire, rescue, state police and other emergency services. As far as she was aware, the office from which she was calling was in the path of the flood, but she never once gave any thought to abandoning her post. She was truly one of the heroes of this disaster. Thankfully, her life was spared.

DEPUTY PAUL NESTER

Paul Nester was a real-life character who, at the time of the dam disaster, was a deputy sheriff assigned to Temple Station. He had previously been assigned to the Newhall Station. When the dam broke, he was ordered to offer whatever assistance he could in the rescue and recovery efforts.

In later life he wrote an autobiography that describes, not only his experiences as a deputy sheriff, but several other adventures as well. The book is entitled FIRST HALF OF MY LFE.

SOLEDAD LUNA

It took several days, or perhaps weeks, for the Luna family to reunite.

It was a bitter sweet-reunion for Soledad. While she felt blessed that her mother, father and siblings had all survived the ordeal, she felt a terrible sense of loss at the deaths of her cousins. They had been her playmates, as well as an integral part of her family. The bodies of four of her cousins had been found buried in the mud left by the flood. The body of the fifth cousin, Consuelo, was never found.

In addition to having no home to which they might return, the almost total destruction of the orchards left the migrants with no means of income. The plight of all of them was ominous, but these migrants were a resilient people. And they managed to survive.

Soledad would grow up to become an attractive woman. She would live, for a time, with her grandparents, though it is unknown to the author where that home was located. Throughout her life she was reluctant to relate her experience during the flood. The memories were haunting, though she never forgot the name of Mr. Baxter, to whom she owed so much.

She would live a long life, passing away in 2017, a few months before reaching her one hundredth birthday.

IT SHOULD ALSO be mentioned that there were no meaningful records as to how many migrant workers were actually lost in the flood. The migrants tended to come and go – work a few days then move on to other parts of the state. They would be replaced by other workers seeking employment. Their coming and going generally went unnoticed. It was next to impossible to obtain a record of the total number of migrants working in the valley on any given day. Therefore, the actual count of migrant lives lost is unknown, but it is almost certain that the total number of deaths far exceeded four hundred.

RECOMMENDED READING

WILLIAM MULHOLLAND And the Rise of Los Angeles – by Catherine Mulholland

MAN-MADE DISASTER The Story of St. Francis Dam – by Charles Outland

MY LIFE EAST AND WEST – by William S. Hart

BISCAILUS Sheriff of the New West – by Lindly Bynum and Idwall Jones

FIRST HALF OF MY LIFE – by Paul Nester

VISION OR VILLAINY Origins of the Owens Valley-Los Angeles Water Controversy By Abraham Hoffman

RIVERS IN THE DESERT William Mulholland and the inventing of Los Angeles By Margaret Leslie Davis

WATER AND POWER By William L. Kahrl

CADILLAC DESERT The American West and Its Disappearing Water
By Mark Reisner

Printed in the USA
CPSIA information can be obtained
at www.ICGtesting.com
LVHW052320171124
796831LV00001B/185

*9 7 8 1 9 5 8 8 9 2 7 9 4 *